Nashville ER

Saving lives and healing hearts!

After a busy shift at Nashville's
Saint Dolores Hospital, aka St. Dolly's,
Avery Whittacker and Lia Costa love nothing
more than meeting up for gossip, guacamole and a
pitcher of margaritas. The friends agree on almost
everything, including that neither has room in her
life for romance…

But the New Year brings two new doctors to their
busy ER, who make waves in the department and
set the friends' hearts fluttering!

Nurse practitioner Avery Whittacker isn't
looking for love, until one of St. Dolly's
newest MDs, Carter Booth, gets under her skin
and into her heart, in:

New Year Kiss with His Cinderella
By Annie O'Neil

Vascular surgeon Lia Costa is perfectly happy
focusing on her career, until Dr. Micah Corday
comes back into her life—a decade after she broke
both their hearts by sending him away, in:

Their Reunion to Remember
By Tina Beckett

Dear Reader,

Have you ever met an old acquaintance and not recognized them immediately? There's that whole "Hi there, how are you?" exchange that leaves you scrambling to identify the person. What if that awkward moment was something you struggled with every single day?

For vascular surgeon Lia Costa, that is life. Due to a childhood illness, she can no longer recognize faces, a condition called prosopagnosia. It affects every aspect of her life. When she runs into a former lover on Valentine's Day, she is stumped for a few brief seconds as to who he is. But that moment proves to be a pivotal event that rocks her world.

Thank you for joining Lia and Micah as they attempt to resolve their past issues and find a way to redefine what is important…and what is not. It won't be easy, but maybe, just maybe, they will discover something they thought they'd lost.

I hope you love reading about these two special characters as much as I loved writing their story.

Love,

Tina Beckett

THEIR REUNION
TO REMEMBER

TINA BECKETT

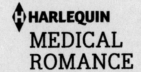

HARLEQUIN
MEDICAL
ROMANCE

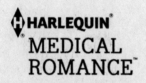

HARLEQUIN®
MEDICAL
ROMANCE™

Recycling programs
for this product may
not exist in your area.

ISBN-13: 978-1-335-40900-3

Their Reunion to Remember

Copyright © 2021 by Tina Beckett

This edition published by arrangement with Harlequin Books S.A.

For questions and comments about the quality of this book,
please contact us at CustomerService@Harlequin.com.

Harlequin Enterprises ULC
22 Adelaide St. West, 41st Floor
Toronto, Ontario M5H 4E3, Canada
www.Harlequin.com

Printed in U.S.A.

Three-times Golden Heart® Award finalist **Tina Beckett** learned to pack her suitcases almost before she learned to read. Born to a military family, she has lived in the United States, Puerto Rico, Portugal and Brazil. In addition to traveling, Tina loves to cuddle with her pug, Alex, spend time with her family and hit the trails on her horse. Learn more about Tina from her website, or friend her on Facebook.

Books by Tina Beckett

Harlequin Medical Romance

The Island Clinic collection

How to Win the Surgeon's Heart

New York Bachelor's Club

Consequences of Their New York Night
The Trouble with the Tempting Doc

A Summer in São Paulo

One Hot Night with Dr. Cardoza

A Christmas Kiss with Her Ex-Army Doc
Miracle Baby for the Midwife
Risking It All for the Children's Doc
It Started with a Winter Kiss
Starting Over with the Single Dad

Visit the Author Profile page
at Harlequin.com for more titles.

To my husband, who truly makes me feel seen.

PROLOGUE

ILIANA COSTA STARED at the lineup of fathers, her insides beginning to unravel in panic. She tried to remember what Papa had told her to do in a situation like this. But it wasn't working. From this distance, she couldn't spot the small scar at the outside corner of his left eye, and right now all the dark-haired men blurred into one indistinct subset of humans with no defining features. No way to tell them apart other than by their clothes. And she had no idea what Papa was wearing.

She glanced at her classmates, who—with a chicken egg perched on each of their spoons—were laughing and anxious to race toward one of the men on the other side of the room.

Lia was not laughing. All she felt was fear and the remembrance of being made fun of for going to the wrong person. It had happened so many times. With teachers. With friends. With her mom and dad. The worst had been at a mother/daughter tea when she'd gone up and sat with the wrong mom at one of the fancy tables. A little girl had come up to her, chest puffed out and declared that was *her* mother and that Lia couldn't have her. Every head had turned to stare at her. And then came the whispers. Her own mom, who'd arrived late, had come over and rescued her.

It was why her mother now wore a stretchy pink bracelet around her wrist, so that Lia could spot her from a distance. She remembered fingering that bracelet when she was nervous. It was harder with her father, who'd insisted she learn to recognize him using means other than his face. So she used the scar beside his eye. It was his tell…his pink bracelet.

Why didn't other kids have this problem?

Two of the men had beards, so she mentally marked them off the list. One was much taller than the others. Not him, either.

The whistle sounded, and the girls took off, each choosing a direction with a certainty that Lia didn't understand. She ran, too, desperately searching through the rest of the dads, looking for a clue. Then one of the men locked eyes with her, his left hand slowly coming up and forming a thumbs-up sign.

Papa! Oh, Papa, thank you!

Taking a grateful breath, she fixed her gaze on him and changed directions, moving toward him with a sureness she didn't feel. Until she got closer and saw that familiar scar.

Then she knew. *This* man was her father. Her heart swelled with love, the fear slowly trickling away.

When she reached him, she carefully transferred her egg from her spoon to his. And as he moved away from her toward the starting line, her gaze followed his every step, memorizing the clothing he had on. Dark blue shirt. Black pants. Rubber-soled shoes.

Then and only then could she relax with the knowledge that she wouldn't lose him again.

Not until next time, when her sorting process would begin all over again. Just like it did each and every day of her life.

CHAPTER ONE

THE SINGER AT the Valentine's Day benefit concert had something combustible going on with the guitar player seated next to her. It smoldered in the dark glances she sent his way. Sizzled in how he hunched over his guitar, fingers stroking the strings of that hourglass-shaped instrument as if she were on the receiving end of his touch. And the flames they generated spread to the audience as well, who sat forward in their chairs as if they couldn't get enough. As the plaintive notes of a love song cast its spell, Micah Corday perused the space, looking for a vacant seat.

He knew all about spells. Man, did he ever. But hell, he was older and wiser and had no time for those kinds of games anymore. It had been three years and a whole lot of mileage since he'd last been in this town.

The atmosphere here in Nashville was so

different from Ghana, where he'd landed after a breakup. These people were not worried about their next meal or where they'd find clean water or medicine. Instead, their attention was fixed on what was happening on that stage. And between the musicians on it.

But despite that, every one of these folks had their own problems. Their own fears. That part was not so different.

His eyes continued wandering, landing on one face after another before a tingle of remembrance forced him to retrace his steps, first mentally and then emotionally.

There. He found her.

Damn. Talk about spells. He'd known there was a possibility she'd still be in the area, that he'd eventually run into her. But he'd hoped it would come later than this. When he'd had time to frame his questions about that time.

Maybe she was just revisiting her alma mater?

Her eyes were closed, and she swayed slightly to the music, but he knew exactly what color would emerge when her lids parted. Tawny tones that seemed to hold the mystery of the ages. He could remember the way that gaze had held his as she studied him in minute detail until he felt nothing was hidden from her.

It had been like that as they sat across from each other on a dinner date. As she'd straddled his hips and carried him to the very edges of sanity. It had been what had attracted him to her. The details she noticed. Details that had nothing to do what other women saw when they looked at his face. It had been...different. She saw what others missed.

At one time, he'd been so sure of everything. Of his feelings. Of hers. Of the certainty they would someday marry. Have kids.

Until graduation day, when those warm eyes had turned chilly with rejection. There'd been no explanation. No hint as to what had gone wrong.

The memory of that moment—of the strained goodbyes—made something harden in his chest. He'd had no idea what had happened. But once done, there'd been no undoing it. His pride had taken a huge hit that day. He'd evidently thought things were more serious between them than she had. He'd made certain he never made that mistake again. With anyone. His few encounters while on medical mission had been short and sweet. No unrealistic expectations. Then again, he hadn't felt the pull that he had with Lia.

Was she married now?

It didn't matter. What did matter was whether or not she was practicing medicine here at the hospital or just visiting. If it was the former, he would be working under the same roof as her, if not on the same floor.

So, best to get his facts straight now, before they met by chance in a crowded elevator. Or, worse, over a patient.

With that in mind, he moved toward her.

Lia sensed a presence.

Her eyes opened and she took in the stage, where Avery was still singing, both hands wrapped around her microphone as if needing the support. She knew how hard it had been for her friend to get up on that stage. But wow, it had been so worth it. Lia was proud of her.

The hairs on her nape sent an alert, reminding her why she'd opened her eyes in the first place. Her gaze swung to the right and saw a man staring at her from a couple of rows ahead. He was actually walking in her direction. She blinked, quickly tracking across his face, although she wasn't sure why. That never did any good. A vague sense of panic washed over her when he didn't break eye contact and continued coming toward her.

Maybe he was heading for someone else.

No. He stopped. Right in front of where she sat at the end of her row.

Her thoughts gathered around her in quick snatches, and she finally grabbed hold of the one that held her in good stead most of the time. "Hi. How *are* you?" She infused an enthusiasm into the greeting that fooled most people into thinking she'd recognized them.

His head cocked, a frown appearing between his brows.

Uh-oh. It evidently hadn't fooled him.

"Lia? It's Micah. Micah Corday?"

The second his voice sounded, a sick vibration shuddered through her stomach. *Dio.* Of course it was. How could she *not* have recognized him, of all people? He'd been her lover through most of medical school. And at one time she'd thought, maybe just this once, she would finally be able to...

But of course she couldn't. If anything, this moment in time told her her decision back then had been the right one. The instant flash of hurt in his eyes when he'd had to identify himself had provided proof of that.

She'd almost told him her secret back then. But fear had her putting off that moment time and time again. And then graduation had come, snatching up all her hopes and dreams and crushing them into dust.

She jumped to her feet and grabbed him in a quick hug, realizing immediately the imprudence of that move when his scent wrapped her in bittersweet memories. The stubble on his cheek scraped across her skin in a way that rekindled a forgotten spark in her heart and set it alight. Her breath caught on a half sob when he stiffened under the close contact.

Of course he wouldn't welcome her embrace. Why would he?

Swallowing down the ball of emotion, she took a step back. "I—I thought you were in Ghana."

"I was. I'm back."

Her tongue ran across her parched lower lip, trying to think of a response to that shocking statement. "You're back? As in for good?"

His lips curved in a smile that contained not a hint of humor, and Lia could have cried at how hard he seemed. How unlike the Micah she'd once known and loved.

No wonder she hadn't recognized him.

Her heart branded her a liar. That wasn't the reason, and she knew it. It was the same reason she sometimes needed help recognizing her parents. Her friends. Her coworkers.

Faces didn't register with her. Ever. And although medical science had a fancy-sounding name for it, the reality of it was pretty brutal on relationships. Which was why she'd had so few of them in her lifetime.

Her dad's coaching her about how to blend in—done out of love and having had a brother who was bullied in school for a disability—had backfired in some ways. She'd learned with great success how to hide her own challenges, but in doing so had ended up isolating herself. Like choosing a profession where people were in and out of her life in a matter of hours. No need to go to the trouble of remembering details about them. Relationships hovered on a superficial level.

Except with Avery, who had been the only person in her life who could actually joke about her condition. In fact, her closest friend had a scrap of commentary for every person they met: *Ear stud, right ear. Mr. Fancy Pants. Abs galore.* They were funny quips, but they also provided clues for later recognition.

"Yes. As in for good." Micah's voice brought her back to the matter at hand.

She swallowed, her throat aching. *Dio*, she didn't know if she could handle him being back in Nashville. It had taken forever to get used to life without him. Maybe it was better to know exactly what he meant by being back for good.

"Let's go to the back where we can talk." She glanced up at the stage, where Avery continued to sing. For Lia, Avery's hair was her tell. That glorious mane of curls seemed as untamable as her friend. Avery had pulled her safely from some pretty gnarly situations, like when the hospital's chief of staff had ditched his signature pompadour hairstyle in favor of a simple side part and appeared in front of her in shirtsleeves instead of his regular suit and tie. She'd had no idea who he was at first. As if sensing her struggle, her friend had deftly stepped in and greeted him just before he asked Lia about a patient of hers. She'd been grateful beyond words.

But there was no saving her from her current predicament.

She walked to the back of the venue and found a quiet corner. "When did you get back?"

"Yesterday, actually." His smile revealed his tell—the deep, craggy line that appeared in his left cheek whenever his lips curved. That…and that heady masculine scent that no one—in all her years of interacting with men—had been able to match. He used to chuckle at the way she'd press her nose to his skin and breathe deeply, letting the air flow back out on a sigh.

Dio. So many memories. So many moments lost since…

No. She steeled her resolve. She'd been doing him a favor by breaking things off. Although there was no way that he could know that. And that had been the idea. All his talk in the year leading up to graduation about doing a stint with Doctors Without Borders had made her nervous. Leave Nashville? Where it had taken forever to learn to separate the people in her own little bubble of acquaintances? Not likely. But she'd gone along with it, hoping he would change his mind. But he hadn't, as evidenced by his work in Ghana.

But he was back? In Nashville, of all places.

He'd only gotten back yesterday, so maybe that meant he was back for good, as in the United States. Maybe this was a stopping place before he continued on to somewhere else, like…say, Omaha.

"So where are you headed from here?"

"Headed?"

"I just meant…"

Dread filled her heart and permeated the ensuing silence.

"You seriously didn't recognize me?"

The dread grew into something that threatened to burst through the confines of her skin as she scrabbled for an excuse. "You didn't have a beard back then. Or that deep tan. Besides, there's a lot going on, and the last time I saw you…"

"Yes." His smile had disappeared. "The last time you saw me was…well, the last time you saw me."

At graduation.

She remembered that day like it was yesterday. The fear. The horror. As she'd stood in front of that crowd of gowned graduates, she'd been transported back in time to the day when she couldn't pick her father out of a crowd.

She'd flat-out panicked. The orange-and-white robed figures all looked the same, although if she hadn't freaked out and had given herself a minute or two she might have been able to deduce which one of them was Micah. *Might* being the operative word.

The thought of going to a country where she recognized no one—with a man she couldn't even pick out of a crowd—sent her into a tailspin. That, and the growing fear that she one day wouldn't be able to recognize her own child, suddenly morphed into a unscalable wall. What about high school graduation? Ballet class? Baseball games? Any event in which a uniform could disguise identities and steal them from her. Yes. She'd broken things off for all those reasons. And she'd never seen Micah again.

Until today.

She owed him an explanation. But where even to begin…

"I'm sorry. For everything."

His enigmatic eyes searched her features. Seeing what? How had he picked her out from hundreds of other people in the crowd? She would never understand it. "Yeah, well what's done is done. But if we're going to be working at the same hospital…*this* hospital…" His brows went up in question.

"Yes, I work here. As a vascular surgeon."

"Well, then. I guess we'd better figure out what we're going to do about the elephant now standing in the room."

She blinked, thinking maybe he'd figured it out, although her prosopagnosia was something very few people knew about. In fact, Avery was the only person at the hospital who actually knew her little secret. She'd become pretty adept at figuring out who was who. Except when she was caught off guard.

Like by the hospital administrator.

And today, by Micah.

She stood a little taller, her chin tipping up a bit. "And what elephant, exactly, is that?" The word *elephant* slipped out with an accent that belied her Italian heritage. Another quirk brought on by nerves.

"That we were once close. Very, very close."

A sense of relief should have washed over her. Instead, her mouth went dry as a few of those moments of closeness flickered across a screen in her head. The most outrageous being the time they'd had a quickie under a stairwell of this very hospital. They'd been fully clothed, and it had taken just a few minutes, but she'd been left with legs that were shaking and molten memories of the urgency of the act for the rest of the day. *Mio Dio*, if they'd been caught…

She swallowed. "Why does anyone have to know?"

The left side of his mouth cocked, carving out his cheek again. "You don't think anyone knew we were sleeping together back then?"

Okay, so probably a lot of the people they'd known had guessed. And Avery definitely knew, because she'd told her. But once she broke things off with Micah, she'd firmly told her friend she didn't want to hear Micah's name come out of her mouth. Her friend had honored her request over the past three years, never mentioning Micah or what had transpired between them. It had made getting over him a little easier. At least that's what she'd told herself back then.

"I vote we say nothing, other than that we already know each other. And if someone asks, we'll simply say that was in the past and that we've both moved on."

"Moved on. Yes, that's one way of putting it."

Wow, this broody Micah, whose syllables could cut like a scalpel, was going to take some getting used to. But *this* iteration she could handle. If he'd been the mellow, playful guy from her past, she might have had trouble keeping her distance. Might have even repeated mistakes of her past. But this man? Yes. He was a relief. Him she could resist. Could even avoid with ease.

With that thought, she sent him a smile of her own. "Yes. It is one way of putting it. But the terminology doesn't matter. What does is that we're both adults who can work together as professionals." She realized Avery had finished singing and, as a result, her words had come out a lot louder than they might have if the music had still been playing. A couple of people looked in their direction, and she cringed, much like she'd done at that tea party so long ago.

Okay, time to make a quick getaway and find her friend. "There's someone I need to meet, so I'll say goodbye. Enjoy the rest of the benefit."

With that she turned and walked away from him, hoping her steps looked more even than they felt, and vowing she would do everything in her power to make sure they worked together as little as possible.

CHAPTER TWO

AVERY FLAGGED HER down in the hallway first thing Monday morning, making Lia smile. She'd looked for her friend after the Valentine's Day benefit, but both she and her sexy guitar player had vanished. Lia had a feeling she knew why.

"Hey, girlie, sorry I cut out on you at the benefit. But I…uh…had someplace I needed to be."

Her friend's burgeoning relationship with trauma surgeon Carter Booth had been fun to watch unfold, although she knew it had been touch and go for a while.

"You had someplace you needed to be? Or someone you needed to be with?"

"Well…both. And I have some news."

"News? So everything worked out okay?" Lia had a feeling she already knew the answer to that question.

"More than okay. I just never dreamed

I would ever..." She grabbed Lia's hand. "Carter asked me to marry him."

She'd had a feeling this was coming. Things had been heating up between the pair for a while now.

"Oh, honey, I am so, so happy for you!"

Avery deserved to find happiness after everything she'd been through. One good part about Lia's inability to separate one face from another was that she had a knack for reading emotions in others without needing to have them spelled out. And Avery's emotion was there in spades. It was in the grip of her friend's hand on hers. In the tremble to her voice as she'd said that last sentence, as if unable to believe her luck.

That ability to read people made Lia hyperaware of how noticeable her own feelings could be and gave her the tools to stow them out of sight.

Although that ability had ended up causing friction between her and Micah, especially over that last year. Whenever she'd submerged her true feelings about signing up with Doctors Without Borders, he'd seemed to sense something was wrong and pushed until she snapped at him that everything was fine. Even when it wasn't. The look he used to give her when she did that stayed with her even now. As if he was so disappointed in her. It had ripped at her heart.

Another good reason to have broken it off. And seeing him again had brought up a lot of emotions she'd thought were long dead.

"I have some news of my own." She looked her friend in the eye. "Remember that name I asked you never to mention?"

Avery's eyes widened. "You mean Slash and Burn?"

Her friend's nickname for Micah made her roll her eyes. Avery had once said that every time that slash appeared in Micah's left cheek, Lia would turn beet red. And she had.

But unlike Avery, who looked like she'd gotten everything she ever dreamed of— her return to singing, finding a man who understood her and loved her for who she was—Lia didn't expect Micah's sudden appearance to cause anything but renewed heartache.

"Yes. Micah." She bit her lip. "He's back in Nashville."

"No! For real?"

"Unfortunately."

"Couldn't this be a good thing? Sometimes things happen for a reason."

Her friend's optimism probably sprang from cloud nine, the place where Avery was currently perched. She was happy, therefore everyone she loved deserved happiness, too. Unfortunately it didn't always work out that way.

"Don't get any ideas. We're not getting back together. That's not what I want." She ignored the little voice inside her that warned her pants were now on fire. "I just wanted you to know, in case you see him around the hospital."

"He's going to be *working* here?" Avery let go of her hand. "How do you feel about that?"

"It's awkward. He came up to me at the benefit and said he had come back to work."

"Did he say why?"

"I was so shocked, I didn't even think to ask. Just got away from him as fast as I could." She swallowed. "Ave, I didn't even recognize him when he came up to me."

"I'm so sorry. But you had no idea he was here—was probably the last person you expected to see at the benefit."

Yes, that was true. But any other person would have known immediately if an ex-lover came and stood in front of them.

"At least we won't cross each other's paths

all that often. I'm in ER for the most part, and he'll be...well, I'm not exactly sure, but probably up in the lab area." She forced a smile. "Anyway, enough about Micah. I'm really am happy for you. You deserve all that and more."

"Thanks. I love Carter to pieces." She seemed to hop down off her cloud. "But that's actually not why I came down to find you. Has a woman named Bonnie Chisholm been in contact with you this morning to make an appointment?"

"The name doesn't sound familiar. Why?"

She sighed. "She's had some problems going on, and I'm worried she's a stroke risk. I asked her a couple of weeks ago to call you, but she evidently didn't, since she called me again last night with a new symptom." There was a pause. "She was my sister's and my singing teacher. She's...special to me."

"Can you give me some details?"

Avery quickly ran down the list of symptoms Bonnie had been having, saying she was now having abdominal pains on top of the leg swelling and shortness of breath she'd had two weeks ago.

"She promised me she'd call you today."

"I haven't heard from her. She does need to see a specialist. If not me, then another vascular surgeon. Maybe she's worried. Any chance you could come in with her?"

"I offered to. I'll go talk to her again. I'll admit, I'm the one who's worried. She's one of the main reasons I got up on that stage at the benefit."

Lia smiled. "And here I thought that was due to my nagging. Or maybe due to that handsome cowboy who was up there with you."

"It was definitely a group effort." She glanced at her phone, which had just buzzed. "Damn. Sorry, I need to run. One of my patients needs my help."

"Go, I'll catch up with you later. Thursday night for guac and talks? If you can pull yourself away from Carter, that is." Their weekly meet up had become a tradition neither of them wanted to break. It was a time when they could vent, laugh and just generally unload about their week while enjoying the noisy, saloon-like atmosphere of Gantry's Margarita Den.

"Carter knows I need my weekly dose of the best guac east of the Mississippi, so yes, Thursday is great."

Her friend was positively glowing. Maybe someday she would find what Avery seemed to have found. But for now, she would live vicariously through her friend's romance. "See you then."

Avery gave a wave as she hurried back toward the ER.

Her friend knew about Micah and Lia's reasons for breaking things off three years ago, although Avery had pooh-poohed her fears about going on medical mission and about not recognizing her own child. She'd assured her that when the right guy came along, those fears would slide away.

But would they really? Lia had been so sure that Micah was that person. And she'd half wondered if she'd let the one get away. Until Micah had shown up at the gala after his long absence and Lia hadn't recognized him. As much as she tried to blame that on shock or the unexpectedness of his face coming back across her radar, it simply re-affirmed all her reasons for breaking off the relationship.

How fitting that she worked at Saint Dolores, who was the patron saint of sorrows. In Italian, *doloroso* meant sorrowful or painful. Both of those terms aptly described her feelings about ending things with Micah. There was still some *grande dolore* involved when she thought about him.

And now that he was here?

She was going to concentrate on seeing him as a colleague. Someone who meant nothing to her anymore. No pain. No sadness. No longing. If her dad's job as a molecular biologist had taught her one thing, it was that things could be broken down to a scientific set of molecules. Those molecules could then be manipulated to change the way they came together. So if she could change one of the building blocks that had made her want to be with Micah, she could change the entirety of their relationship and make it into something else—something that worked on a professional level but not a deeper emotional level. She just needed to find which of those blocks she needed to change to make that happen.

And if she couldn't? Then the name Saint Dolores was going to be a daily reminder of the hurt she had gone through when Micah had turned and walked away from her, head held high, strong shoulders braced to face life without her.

And from all appearances, he'd done a very good job of doing just that.

She only hoped she'd done just as good a

job. Because if not, *dolore* was going to be a hard word to shake. And an even harder emotion to outrun.

"There's someone I need to meet."

Those words had echoed again and again in Micah's subconscious over the weekend. And they were making his first day on the job pretty damned rough.

He thought his pride had taken a hit at their breakup? Well, it was going to take an even bigger hit if Lia had found someone who could give her what he evidently lacked. Every time he thought of her with another man, the crunching blow of a sledgehammer seemed to knock against his ribs.

Hell, the woman had barely even known who he was at the Valentine's benefit, despite their steamy past. So it was ridiculous to even care one way or the other.

Except he was rethinking coming back to the States. Lia's reaction was a stark reminder of his childhood, when he'd felt completely invisible to two busy parents who'd handed him over to a series of nannies. He used to wonder as a kid if they would even recognize him in a crowd.

Ha! Well, he'd seen firsthand that it truly was possible to forget what someone you used to love looked like. It wasn't a fun feeling.

Unless Lia had been faking it, trying to appear nonchalant as she processed the shock of seeing him again.

No. The shock when she realized who he was hadn't been feigned. Neither had the dismay that followed right on its heels, despite her wiping both emotions from her face a second later. Something else she'd been good at when they'd been together, and another thing she had in common with his folks: hiding her true feelings.

A knock sounded on the door to his office just as he reached into a box of books he'd been unpacking onto a shelf. "Come in."

The door opened and a face that he would never forget as long as he lived peered in at him, eyes wary and unsure. She edged inside the door and shut it behind her, leaning against it as if she was ready to rip it open and disappear at the first sign of trouble. Her eyes tracked over his face, seeming to study it before moving on to his body. He remembered how her gaze used to feel like a physical touch and how strangely it had affected him the first time they met.

It was no different this time. But Micah was different. He'd been inoculated against that intense stare. At least he thought he had. "Hello, Lia. Can I help you?" He made his voice as cool and indifferent as he could.

She nodded at the book in his hand. "Well, that seems apropos."

Glancing down, he took in the title. *Preventing Recurrence: It's Up to You.*

"I'm not sure I follow."

"Oh, well, I…um, wanted to talk to you about working together. I know it's going to be weird, but I hope we can somehow figure it out."

He still didn't see how the book… Oh. She wanted to make sure he knew there wouldn't be a recurrence of what had happened between them. No worries there. Because he had no intention of allowing what had happened before to happen again. And she was right. The title was apropos. Because it was up to him—up to them—to make sure that it didn't. "I'm sure we can. Our relationship ended years ago. If you're worried I might be interested in rekindling things, you needn't bother. You made it quite clear that it was a mistake. And I came to realize you were right. We both dodged a bullet."

Her eyes widened before she nodded. "Yes, I think we did. Both of us. I think there's only one person at the hospital who knows we were once an item. And I'd prefer to keep it that way."

"There's not much chance of me broadcasting it over Saint Dolores's loudspeakers."

She seemed to cringe away from that. "I didn't think you would. I just didn't want you to worry about any gossip I might spread."

His smile was hard. "There wouldn't be much to spread. Not anymore."

"No. I guess not."

When that hammer swung against his ribs again, he quickly turned to put the book on the shelf behind his desk. "I agree that we are the key to making this work. So let's just keep our past where it belongs—in the past. There's no reason for anyone to know that we once dated each other."

"And if they ask?"

He turned back to her. "Why would they? I'm new to the hospital, as far as most people know. Would you wonder if I used to date any of Saint Dolores's other employees?"

"Saint Dolly's."

"Sorry?"

"This is Nashville. Surely you remember the nickname we've given the place?"

He'd forgotten about the hospital's second name. "Is that what you call it in front of patients?"

"No, I just…well, Saint Dolly's sounds a little more cheerful than Dolores." She looked down at her clasped hands. "And you might wonder if you heard a bunch of people use the other moniker."

"Okay, Saint Dolly's. Check. Keeping our past a secret. Check." He motioned to the box on his desk. "Anything else?"

"I, um…" Her head came up. "Actually, yes. Why here?"

Was she really asking him that?

"Why did I decide to come here? Why not? It's where I grew up. Where my—" his jaw tightened "—parents live."

"Of course. Sorry. I'm not sure why I asked that."

Did she think he'd come here to restart their romance? Not hardly. If anything, it was the opposite of that. His dad wasn't well, but that wasn't the only reason he was here. He'd come back to the place where his folks lived as a reminder of what it felt like to be invisible. A reminder to be on his guard against getting involved with some- one who made him feel like they'd made him feel. Like Lia had when she'd ended their relationship.

And like when she hadn't recognized him at the benefit. Lia was a much more vivid and present image of what he'd gone through in his childhood. And now he wasn't sure he needed a daily reminder of that to keep him on his toes. Actually, he was sure of it.

"Not a problem." He was hoping those words would prove to be prophetic. "If it helps, I had no idea you were working here when I applied for the job."

"It doesn't help. Not really. But it is what it is. Like you said, we'll find a way to make it work." Her brows went up. "And my parents still live here, too. That's why I've stuck around. Besides, I love it here. I can't imagine practicing medicine anywhere else."

"I think you made that pretty obvious." Part of her little speech the night of graduation had revolved around the idea that they both wanted different things out of life. Except he hadn't realized that. Not until that night.

Right now he was wishing he hadn't been quite so quick to leave Africa. He'd done some real good there, but his mom's phone call saying that his dad's health was beginning to fail had prompted him to come home. Although he still hadn't gone to see them. This week, though, he would make it a point to stop in and see if they needed anything.

"And I have no intention of trying to convince you to go anywhere else. Not anymore."

She stepped away from the door, and for a second he thought she was going to move toward him. Instead, she half turned and twisted the doorknob. "Well, now that we've established some ground rules, I'll let you get back to unpacking."

Had they established that? Or had they just agreed that they could be grown-ups and work together? Well, he wasn't going to say anything that might encourage her to hang around his office any longer than necessary.

"Thanks for coming by."

She gave a half-hearted smile and nodded. "Thanks for understanding." With that, she was through the door, quietly closing it behind her. Micah was left with an office that looked exactly like it had before she'd put in an appearance. The space inside his chest was a different story, however. There were traces of her visit painted on almost every internal surface. His gut. His chest wall. His heart.

And like with most infections, sometimes all it took was a minute amount to put some-

one's life in jeopardy. So he needed to eradi-
cate every stray cell that she'd implanted in
him. He thought he'd done that.

The problem was, now that he was back,
he wasn't quite sure he had.

CHAPTER THREE

LIA PUSHED THROUGH the doors of the ER on her way to the parking lot where her car was located. She'd had three difficult surgeries in a row and was worn out. Just as she was about to step off the curb, a car pulled up and a woman leaped out. "Are you a doctor?"

She blinked, then realized her lanyard was still hanging around her neck. "I am. What's going on?"

"It's my baby." She threw open the back door, where a chilling sound reached Lia. Coughing. But not the normal cough of bronchitis or a respiratory infection. This was a strangled gasping sound she would never in her life forget. "She just had a cold. It was just a cold." Her words were filled with fear and dread.

An infant who couldn't have been older than two months lay propped in a car seat.

"Let's get her inside. But I want to use the side door." She glanced at the mom. "Were you vaccinated against whooping cough while carrying her?"

The woman's face went deadly pale. "No. My doctor mentioned it, but I wasn't vaccinated with my others, and they were fine."

Vaccination during each pregnancy was a fairly new recommendation. The thought was that when the mother passed her antibodies to her fetus, she would pass them along for pertussis as well and hopefully curb the numbers that were slowly creeping up, even in this day and age.

Dio. If she was right?

Lia unbuckled the child, taking in the red, fevered face just as another bout of coughing racked the infant's tiny body. It was followed by the struggle to draw in breath afterward. With the mom racing beside her, they circumvented the double doors and the crowded waiting room and found one of the isolation rooms. "Sit with her for a minute while I do an exam. What's your name?"

"Molly. And this is Sassy."

The mom climbed onto the exam table, her own cough barking out. Damn. Lia donned a mask, not just for her protection but for her patient's. "Are any of your other children sick?"

"All three of them are, but none of them are coughing as much as Sassy."

All of them. "Who's with them?"

"My mom. My husband went to park the car. I've had a cold and just assumed…"

"It's okay." She quickly called down to Admitting to let them know that a man would be coming in and where to direct him. She also asked them to call Micah and a pediatric pulmonologist. So much for not working with her ex. But as an infectious disease expert, Micah needed to know that there might be a possible outbreak of pertussis in one of the local communities.

She listened to the baby's lungs, ignoring her phone when it started buzzing in her pocket. Whoever it was could wait.

Just as she thought—the baby's airways were clogged. "I need to get a swab. If it's whooping cough, we'll need to check your other children, and you'll need to alert any kids you've been in contact with."

"Oh, God. My sister came over with her kids three days ago. Her newest is even younger than Sass."

"Were any of them sick?"

"No." The poor woman's voice was miserable.

Within a minute, a man poked his head in. "Are you the dad?"

"Yes, I'm Roger Armour. Is she okay?"

Molly held her hand out, her husband going over to grasp it. Okay, Molly had straight dark hair and her husband had blondish hair that was cropped close. The dad also had a tattoo of some kind of fish on his forearm. She submitted those facts to memory in case she needed to recognize them later. "She might have whooping cough."

His head tilted sideways. "Isn't that extinct?"

"I'm afraid it hasn't been eradicated. Not yet."

It was amazing how many people thought the disease had gone the way of smallpox, when it was still here. Still threatening the lives of young children.

A nurse came in, and Lia handed her the swabs that she'd put in protective cases, which she'd labeled with the baby's name. "Could you run those to the lab and ask them to put a rush on it? Possible pertussis."

"Right away."

She'd just left the room when another man

poked his head in. Short blond hair, although the mask obscured his lower face. "Hey, I tried to call."

The voice immediately identified him as Micah. Motioning him in, she said, "Possible case of pertussis." She glanced at Molly. "I think you may have it as well. We need to start you both on a course of erythromycin."

"Did I give it to Sass?"

She understood the mother's angst, but sending her down the path of self-blame would help no one. "It could have come from anywhere. Let's just concentrate on helping you both feel better." She glanced at Roger. "We'll want to treat you as well, just in case, since you've been exposed."

Micah came over and did his own examination. He nodded. "The signs are there. Labs?"

"Just sent them off."

"Great. We'll need to try to do a contact trace."

Some of Lia's neighbors had gotten whooping cough when she was a teen, and the sound of a coughing baby being strolled down the building's hallways had haunted her for years. One day, the baby left and never returned, and she'd been told by her mom that the infant had died at the hospital later that day. She needed to do something besides just sit here and wait for more patients to be brought in.

"I'd like to make up some flyers to alert folks of a possible outbreak."

"Flyers. Good idea."

There was something in his voice that made her look at him. "You don't think so?"

His glace met hers. "I do. Just wishing we'd had the luxury of those when I was in Ghana."

"Right." She couldn't imagine what he'd seen in his years in Africa. But she was pretty sure whooping cough was right up there. Had she been wrong not to go with him? She shrugged off the thought. There was no going back. Not that she wanted to. She'd made the right decision. Both for her and for him.

The baby coughed again, only this time when she tried to breathe back in, there was only a thin whistle of air. "She's not getting enough oxygen. We need to intubate."

Micah lifted the child from the mother, who sobbed and clutched her husband's hand. He moved the baby over to one of the nearby counters while Lia found an intubation kit designed for infants.

Things were tense for a few minutes while they got the tube into place. Attaching an Ambu bag, he glanced at the mom. "I'm sorry, but we'll need to use that bed to transport her."

"Oh, of course!" Molly scrambled down and sank into her husband's waiting arms. "Can we go with her?"

"Sit tight for just a few minutes while we stabilize her." Placing the infant's still form onto the exam table, they unlocked the wheels and rolled her out. "We'll send someone for you as soon as we can."

Once outside the room, Lia directed him the back way to a set of service elevators, where there was the least amount of foot traffic. "We'll get her up in one of the PICU rooms and institute droplet isolation."

Once in the elevator, the only sound was the squeeze of the Ambu bag as Lia checked the baby's vitals for the third time. "She's hanging in there."

"This is kind of outside your specialty, isn't it?"

Lia couldn't tell from his tone if he was ticked that she had called him in or not. "It is, but I was there when the car pulled up, and all the other ER docs were busy with patients. Sorry for calling you, but—"

"You did the right thing."

She relaxed, glancing at him and reading

nothing but concern in his demeanor. He hadn't changed much, outside of his hair and beard, and she again was shocked that she hadn't recognized him right off. But it had happened before, and she was pretty sure it wouldn't be the last time she'd be confused by someone's identity. Especially if it had been a while since she'd seen them. And three years was definitely a while.

Checking the baby's color as the elevator stopped on the third floor, they found Newell Jensen, one of the pediatric specialists, waiting for them. Micah nodded at Lia to fill him in on what had happened so far. She did so with a calmness in her voice that belied the shakiness of her limbs. Whether that was from being in close proximity to Micah or from the immediateness of the emergency, she had no idea. But she had to admit she was glad to hand the baby over to someone whose specialty this actually was. "Her mom and dad are waiting down in ER. They're pretty worried."

"So am I, from the looks of her. Let's get her into a room."

Almost immediately there was a flurry of activity as Sassy was hooked up to a ventilator and her vitals were taken yet again. "We're still waiting on her labs, but from the way she sounded in the ER, I'm pretty sure it's pertussis. Two families have been exposed so far. And I suspect there are more."

"Not good. Let's start her on a course of erythromycin while we wait for confirmation from the lab." Newell glanced at them. "I'll have someone update her parents. Can you notify administration? I'll call the CDC."

"Yes."

The specialist was dismissing them, not because he was being a jerk, but because he had work to do and didn't have time to stand around and talk. Lia could appreciate that.

She and Micah walked back to the elevators, stripping their masks and gloves as they did so and dropping them into a waste receptacle. "Did you see a lot of this when you were in Africa?"

"I was actually there helping with the trachoma outbreaks."

She turned to face him. "Trachoma? As in from chlamydia?"

"One and the same."

She'd had no idea that's what he'd been doing there. Once they broke up, there'd been no need to keep in contact with each other. And for the first time, she wished they had, or that she'd at least kept track of

his career. Then maybe that whole embarrassing scene at the Valentine's Day benefit
wouldn't have happened.

"Why did you come back to the States?"

His lips twisted to the side in a way that
was heartbreakingly familiar.

"Two reasons. My dad and politics."

"Okay, those are two things I never would
have put together. Is your dad running for
office?"

"No." He sighed. "He hasn't been well
for the last year or so. He has cancer, and I
wasn't sure how much longer he was going
to be around. If I was going to visit, now
was the time."

"I'm sorry. I didn't know."

"It's okay. We haven't exactly been close."

She nodded. "I remember you saying that.
Did they even come to your graduation?"

One brow went up. "No. But they sent a
representative. With a very expensive gift."

Reaching out to touch his hand, she murmured, "I'm so sorry, Micah." She hadn't
done a very good job of timing her little
breakup speech, had she?

"It's okay. You didn't know."

Fortunately he didn't add that she hadn't
bothered to stick around to find out, although he must have thought it at the time.

He'd been hurt by everyone he cared about that day. And it made something inside her cramp. If she'd known his mom and dad hadn't come to see him graduate from medical school, would she have broken up with him when she did? She didn't know. And it was too late to go back and change it now that she did. "I'm still sorry. Is there any hope for your dad?"

"I think my dad thinks that cancer is beneath him. That he'll somehow buy his way out from under it, like he's done with most things in his life." He sighed. "And no. According to my mom, he's been given little hope, although he's slated to start an experimental treatment sometime soon."

"Have you talked to him?"

"Not yet. But I'm planning to this weekend."

She could understand his reluctance, but if it had been one of her parents, she would have rushed home as soon as her plane landed. When she and Micah had been together, she'd known that things between him and his parents had been strained, but she'd had no idea it was as bad as it evidently was. He'd never taken her home to meet them, which she hadn't thought was odd at the time, but now that a few years had passed… Had she not noticed out of self-ishness? Out of not wanting to know anything about Micah other than how he made her feel?

Dio, she hoped not.

"I'm sure that will be hard." The elevator stopped and she stepped off, waiting for him to exit as well.

"A lot of things in life are hard. But you somehow get through them and move on."

For some reason she didn't think he was still talking about his parents, and a trickle of remembered pain went through her. She knew he'd been hurt when she'd broken things off, but how much more hurt would he have been when he realized why she had such trouble putting names to faces—including his? She'd been able to laugh it off at the time, saying she was terrible with names. But it wasn't the names that stumped her. It was the faces that went with them.

Even his.

She remembered how hurt she'd been when her dad insisted time and time again that she learn a way to get around her prosopagnosia. He'd never let her take the easy way out…except for during that egg and spoon race. But once she hit high school, she finally understood why. He was protect-

ing her from what his younger brother—
her uncle—had gone through. Her uncle
had been born with a speech impediment
that got him ridiculed again and again, and
her dad had made sure he was always there
to protect his younger brother from bullies.
And when he'd had a daughter who couldn't
recognize faces, he'd stepped back into the
role of protector. It had changed her life for
the better and had been a turning point in
their relationship. But it had also made her
very aware of what could happen if she let
people see behind her curtain.

Evidently things were still strained between Micah and his parents, but maybe
they would have their own turning point
someday. Only if his dad was as ill as he'd
indicated, there might not be much time to
make things right.

Micah had been right to come back.

They made their way to the administra-
tive office, and she spoke in hushed tones to
the hospital administrator's assistant. "We
had an infant come in with a suspected case
of pertussis. Can we get in to see Arnie?"

Arnold Goff headed up the hospital much
like the boxer he'd once been—deftly feint-
ing away from any opponent before coming
back with a hard right hook. Other hospital

administrators treated him with respect. But the man was also fiercely loyal to his staff.

Arnie's assistant picked up his phone and let him know they were here to see him. "He said to go on in."

They went through the door, and the administrator stood to shake their hands. "You must be Dr. Corday. Nice to finally meet you in person."

"A pleasure."

Arnie hadn't been at the hospital while they had attended medical school there, which was kind of a relief. "So what brings you in?"

"We have a case of suspected whooping cough—an infant—although the labs aren't in yet." Lia paused. "The mom is coughing as well and said her other three kids are sick."

"Hell." He motioned them to the two chairs in front of his desk while he sat back down as well. "What do we know?"

She continued. "Not much. Not yet. Not sure where the family was exposed, but they've been with relatives while displaying symptoms."

He dragged a hand through his hair. "Anyone at the hospital exposed?"

"Minimal. I met the couple just as the

mom and baby were getting out of the car. We went in through back doors, and I notified anyone who was going into her room that they needed to don PPE."

"Good thinking. What do you need from me?"

This time Micah spoke up. "Dr. Costa had the idea of putting up flyers around the community alerting the public to the need of reviewing their vaccination records and see if they're up-to-date. The last thing we want in Nashville is a major outbreak of pertussis."

"Agreed. And good thinking. Are you two okay with heading up the push?"

"Us?" Lia's voice came out as a kind of squeak that made Arnie look at her.

"Is there a problem with that?"

"No," she hurried to clarify. "None at all."

The man's gaze moved from one to the other. "I know you both have your own patients, but this is a good opportunity for educating the public, and I can think of no better faces to represent the hospital."

She knew he hadn't meant that comment on faces in the way of grading someone's looks, but it still made her shift in her seat. Because Lia had no idea what made for a more or less attractive set of facial characteristics.

"I'm okay with that as long as Micah has the time."

Too late she realized she'd used his first name rather than his title. But if he noticed, Arnie didn't say anything.

"I don't have anything major scheduled yet. Except this." Micah frowned. "But I'd like to go beyond putting up flyers and see if I can get a handle on where this area stands in the way of vaccinations and contact tracing."

"COVID has given us a little hand up in that area. So hopefully some of those databases can be put to good use."

"That's what I was thinking as well. I can work with the CDC on feeding them whatever info we find out."

Still with the *we*. But then again, she'd have been hurt if Micah had tried to cut her out of the loop, although if he pushed he could have. He was an infectious disease doc, and she was vascular. They weren't quite in the same specialty.

"Can you meet together and come up with a plan and get back to me tomorrow?"

Tomorrow? She'd just been on her way out of work. If she hadn't stopped to assist that cry for help, she'd be home already, soaking in a hot tub. But despite how uncomfortable it might be to pair up with Micah, they'd done fine while treating Sassy. Surely they could handle a couple of hours of planning.

Micah's eyes swung around to meet hers. "Do you have time to discuss it tonight?"

"Sure."

Arnie sighed as if in relief. "Make sure you keep me in the loop."

"Of course." She and Micah said the words in unison.

Lia gave a nervous laugh. That was something they'd always done. And they used to chuckle about it back then. But despite her laugh just now, she didn't find much that was humorous about their current situation.

"I'll leave you to it, then."

She and Micah stood and headed back through the door.

As soon as they were out of earshot, he turned to her. "Sorry about that. I didn't mean to drag you into anything."

"You didn't. The flyers were my idea, re-member?"

"Of course I remember. I wasn't trying to take credit for it."

She smiled. "I didn't think you were. Be-sides, we both want the same thing—to pro-tect the people of Nashville."

"So where do we do this planning?"

"How about over dinner? I'm starved."

He nodded. "Me, too. Any good guacamole joints around here? I seem to remember you having a penchant for the stuff."

And Micah, who hadn't been a fan, had turned into a believer while they were together. And she knew of a very good spot. But it was the place she and Avery frequented for their guac and talks, and she didn't really relish going there. She didn't want his memories sliding around her every time she and Avery walked into the place. Not like a lot of other things in Nashville after they'd broken things off. She'd even thought about leaving town for that very reason, despite the horror of being pushed out of her comfort zone. And now, just when she thought she'd banished all his ghosts, here he came to add new ones. It had made it easier not to go running to him and take back everything she'd said to push him away. And now that he'd returned?

She needed to stand her ground and remember why she'd ended things.

Was she really destined to be alone? Her whole life? She shook off her thoughts. Avery seemingly finding the love of her life made her feel even more alone.

"Guacamole is still the nectar of the gods,

but I'm in the mood for something different. How about wings?"

Although Gantry's Margarita Den also had great wings, there were several other places that sold passable chicken other than her go-to place. And most of them already had…ghosts. Well, she didn't want his ghost inhabiting Gantry's as well. Better for him to roam the kitchen of somewhere that didn't matter to her.

"Sounds good. Is Maurio's still open here in town?"

Maurio's. She hadn't been there since the day before graduation. It was her last wonderful memory of him. Yes. That would be the perfect place, since she purposely didn't go there anymore. And wouldn't go there again after tonight.

"It is. Where are you staying? Or did you already buy something?"

He looked at her. "I haven't bought anything. I'm at a hotel at the moment. They have a shuttle that runs back and forth to the hospital." He shrugged with what looked like an apology. "I haven't gotten a vehicle yet, either."

"It's okay, I can drive and drop you off afterward. Which hotel?"

"Tremont Inn, about three blocks from

the hospital. I figured I could walk to work on days I didn't want to take the shuttle."

"I know where that is. It's right on the way back toward my place."

So with that settled, they headed toward the exit before Micah stopped. "Can I check in and see how Sassy is doing first?"

"I'd thought about doing the same thing, so sure."

With that, they both headed toward the nurses' desk and asked the person behind the desk to page Dr. Jensen.

CHAPTER FOUR

MAURIO'S WAS CROWDED. And loud. Louder than he remembered. The sign at the front of the restaurant told them to "chicken dance to a table of their choice." It had seemed cute back when they were dating. And one time, Lia had actually chicken danced to one of the tables, making him laugh.

They'd been young and in the throes of medical school. Laughing had not been high on the agenda, except when he was with her.

Only the Lia of today didn't look like she'd chicken dance anywhere. She seemed more serious now. Sadder.

Because of him?

She'd broken things off, so maybe. The whys had never been all that clear, though. Looking back, she hadn't seemed all that enthused by the prospect of going on a medical mission with him. But Lia had also been a master at covering up her emotions, withdrawing or pretending to agree instead of sitting down and having a hard conversation. It had irked him and brought back unpleasant childhood memories. Like his parents' glossing over the fact that they really didn't have a relationship with their son. All Lia would have had to do was say no, she didn't want to go overseas, and he would have thought long and hard about going.

But she hadn't.

And she hadn't mentioned it in her breakup speech, which had been short and sweet. In his mind, going after her would have done no good. Instead, it had solidified his decision to follow through with his plans of going with Doctors Without Borders.

Ghana had been an eye-opener on what it was like to practice medicine where supplies were hard to come by. He thought he might go back someday, but right now he wasn't making those decisions. He just needed to get through this time with his parents, then he could look toward the future. Whatever it held.

They found a booth at the very back of the restaurant. Immediately memories danced around him—and they weren't doing anything as humorous as a chicken dance. Instead, they were memories of him and Lia crowded together on the same side of the booth, her foot sliding along his leg and her laughing when his face turned red.

Damn. This was a mistake. And he'd only suggested it because it was first restaurant that had popped into his mind.

Lia didn't sit next to him this time, though. She sat on one side of the table, and he sat on the other. Then again, they were no longer a couple, so it made sense. But it also highlighted the distance between them. One of the waitstaff came over with two menus and put them down in front of them, taking their drink orders. He ordered a beer. It was rare that he drank nowadays, especially after the night of their breakup, when he'd gotten so drunk he couldn't see straight. Literally. He'd used alcohol to try to drown his shock and dismay, but the next day it had come roaring back with a vengeance, along with a hangover that wouldn't quit. He was never going that route again.

But one beer wasn't the same as getting drunk.

She leaned on the table with her elbows rather than sitting way back in her seat, something he remembered from the past. And her hair was up in a ponytail, but the end slid over her shoulder and curled near the swell of her breast. And, hell, if he didn't acutely remember how those same breasts had felt in his hands. He did his best not to follow that train of thought, but it was damned hard.

"You said you haven't seen your folks yet. I'm kind of surprised. Wasn't that why you came back?"

The question came out of nowhere, taking him by surprise. It took him a minute or two to think of a response. Mainly because he wasn't sure why he hadn't gone to see them. His mom knew he was planning on coming home, but he hadn't given her a firm date, preferring to do things on his own terms. His dad had cancer, but it wasn't at the critical point yet. But who knew when that could change? Maybe the experimental treatment his mom had told him about during their phone call wouldn't work.

"It is, but it's been crazy trying to get things set up with work and housing, etc. Once I get a car, it should be easier."

She didn't say anything, just looked at him. And he realized he'd been home for almost a week. Maybe because he knew once he did that seeing his parents would have to take a regular spot on his agenda. And he wasn't quite sure he was ready for that yet.

"My parents and I still don't have the best relationship." The words were out before he could stop them. He knew they sounded weak, but it was the truth, and somehow he'd always had trouble admitting just how bad thing were in his household. Back then he'd told Lia they didn't see eye to eye, but he had never shared what it was that bothered him so much. Maybe because it had seemed selfish of him to want his parents' attention. As if he'd been the only thing on their plates. They were both wildly successful in their careers. They were in demand by myriad people. He was probably just one more person clamoring for their time. He himself had experienced that in Ghana when there were more sick people than there were medical personnel. It had been dizzying, and sometimes he'd just wanted to withdraw from all of it. Had his mom and dad felt that way?

"Yeah, I remember you saying that. I just thought with your dad being sick that things might have gotten better."

The strange thing was, in a way they had. At least from a distance. His mom had emailed him more while he was in Africa than she'd communicated with him the whole time he'd been in medical school. Maybe because it didn't take as much of an emotional investment to type words onto an electronic device as it did when you stood face-to-face with someone.

Like sitting across from Lia again?

Except there was no emotional investment here at all. Not anymore.

"It's complicated."

A good term for it. And for the mixed bag of feelings generated by being at Maurio's again.

Their drinks came, and they gave their meal order to the waiter. Which, strangely, was like being transported back in time. He got the spicy and she got the honey barbecue sauce. It appeared nothing had changed.

Except for them.

Micah took a swig of his beer, his first drink since being back in Nashville. It was smooth going down, the sensation helping to ground him and sweep away some of his misgivings about being here with her.

"And your folks? How are they? Your sister?"

"They're good. My dad is still working for the same medical lab, and my mom is still teaching music. Only she does it from home now. My sister is in Abilene with her husband and kids. When we all get together, it's a mixture of crazy and fun. I adore my nieces."

Her face showed the truth of that statement. The soft smile seemed to come from a place deep inside her.

"And yet you said you weren't sure about having kids of your own."

Her family was so different from his. And when they'd been dating, it was what he'd aspired to. It had given him hope that he could be the kind of dad her father seemed to be. And that he and Lia could have a relationship based on mutual respect and trust, and that they could love their kids—be hands-on parents. And yet she'd been hesitant in her response to his question about how many kids she wanted. It had taken him by surprise. She'd simply said that if practicing medicine was as busy as medical school, she wasn't sure she could give them the attention they deserved. He hadn't pushed. And she hadn't volunteered anything more on that subject.

"My work is pretty fulfilling."

Said as if having a family would make it less so?

He swallowed. That's probably exactly what his parents had felt.

How had he even thought he and Lia had

had the makings of a good relationship? Maybe growing up with apathetic parents had made any kind of emotional attachment seem larger and more meaningful than it actually was. Lia had evidently agreed, since she made it seem like their relationship had been just a phase. Just part of the whole medical school experience.

The aftermath of their breakup had left him reeling. He hadn't had, nor wanted, a relationship since then. He'd trusted Lia with his heart, and she'd handed it back to him without a second thought.

So he'd headed to Ghana rather than face her again. Staying would have been hard. And the last thing he wanted was to find out he was some emotionally needy jerk who couldn't let go.

He was pretty sure he wasn't. Because when he let go, he really let go. Neither he nor Lia had contacted each other again. And although it would have been nice to have true closure, he hadn't gone looking for it. He'd just lost himself in his work.

"I get that kids are hard. I was pretty busy in Ghana, too. Anyway, I'm glad your parents are doing well."

She took a sip of her soda, glancing at him

over the rim before setting it down. "Is there anything I can do to help, Micah?"

It took him a second before he realized she was talking about his parents and not about their past relationship.

"No. I plan to go car shopping after we're done here."

She set her drink down. "I could take you."

"Why?" He stared at her, trying to figure out where this was coming from. Guilt over the past? Surely not.

She shrugged, but the move seemed stiff, as if she was trying to shift some kind of weight from her shoulders, making him think he hadn't been as far off as he'd thought.

"I'm off. You're off. I have a car..." her brows went up "...you don't. Maybe we can kill two birds with one stone and look for places to put up flyers in between stops."

Ah, so that's why. It had had nothing to do with the past.

She went on. "Pertussis is a subject that makes my blood run cold. When I was a kid, a baby in the next apartment had a terrible cough. I was a teenager at the time, and I still vividly remember the sound of it. And the way my parents tried to keep us away from her. But my sister got sick anyway. Not as badly as the baby, but enough to warrant treatment." She fiddled with her napkin. "Anyway, one day I realized the cough in the hallway was gone. Along with the baby. So when Sassy coughed…that sound… It brought up memories I thought were long gone."

He could relate. Not to the pertussis angle, but to the bringing up memories that he thought were long gone.

Every once in a while, he could almost swear he felt a bare foot sliding against his leg, but it was just a phantom ache, like when a part of your body was missing but that you could swear you felt from time to time.

"The baby died."

He didn't know why he'd said it, maybe because a part of him still wanted to understand where Lia was coming from. Despite how close they'd been in medical school, he now realized they'd actually known very little about each other. He'd withheld parts of his past. And evidently she had, too. He'd had no idea her sister had contracted whooping cough.

"Yes. There were a cluster of other cases in the area, which is why I don't want to ignore this. I don't just want to alert the CDC and let them take over. I want make sure Nashville understands the very real dangers of whooping cough."

"I agree." He felt his features soften. "I'm glad your sister pulled through."

She smiled. "Yeah. Me, too. So you see why I really want to be a part of this."

"I do."

They ate their meal, and Micah found himself relaxing, chuckling when a bit of barbecue sauce landed on her cheek. She swiped at it once and missed, and he reached across with his own napkin and rubbed it away. The gesture felt oddly intimate, forcing him to lean back in his seat to detach from it.

"Thanks," she said. "I always seem to do that."

She always had. And he'd always seemed to be the one to fix it back then.

Only he hadn't been able to fix whatever it was that had happened between them at the end. Nor had he tried. His pride had been so stung that he'd simply removed himself from the situation, preferring to lick his wounds in private. Actually, he'd traveled a long distance to make sure he could do exactly that.

He didn't regret going to Ghana. The experience had been fulfilling in a way that was different than what he was doing now at Saint Dolly's.

And right now, Lia was studying him in that crazy way she'd always had and making him feel like nothing had changed.

Except it had. So he averted his eyes and stared at the foam on his beer. "What happened between us back then, Lia?"

He wasn't sure why he'd even asked the question, but once it was out, he couldn't retract it.

There was silence for several long seconds, and when he looked back at her, it was to find she was no longer looking at him. And he found he missed the touch of her gaze. He'd forgotten how much it affected him. Until just now.

"I—I just realized I wasn't ready for a relationship. Not one that involved commitment and sacrifice. I know how much you wanted to work with Doctors Without Borders, and I couldn't…" She shook her head. "I couldn't give you what you needed. What you deserved. I love Nashville. And I didn't want to leave my family."

"You could have told me that." He'd been

right about her reticence to go. "You never know, I might have chosen to stay."

"I knew that was a possibility. And I didn't want to be the reason you didn't go. I had a lot going on at the time, and it seems I made the right decision." She licked her lips. "You never met anyone over there?"

He gave her a slow smile. "I met *lots* of people over there." He kept his meaning ambiguous, although putting the emphasis where he had may have been a little over-the-top. Especially when she bit her lip as if his words had stung.

Damn. He didn't want to say things just to hurt her. He needed to put an end to this conversation, even though he was the one who'd started it. Downing the last of his beer, he waved away the waiter when he asked if he wanted another.

She glanced at him. "Are you sure? I'm driving."

"I'm sure. I was never a big drinker. It's the first beer I've had in a while."

"I remember that about you."

Man, he did not want to go any farther down that road, where they started sharing remembered stories with each other. "Are you sure you want to take me? I can just as easily rent a car."

Except thinking about it, he wasn't sure that was as easy as he'd made it sound. He didn't have auto insurance because...well, no car. Did they even let you rent one without that? He'd never been in that situation before.

"I'm positive. Like I said, we can scout out places to hang flyers." She glanced at her watch. "Most auto dealerships are probably open for another couple of hours, since it's only four. If you're ready to go, that is."

"More than ready."

When they'd checked on Sassy before leaving the hospital, the infant was still holding her own, and the mom and dad had already been started on a course of antibiotics with a stern warning not to go to the store or anywhere else until the whole family had been on them for twenty-four hours.

Micah tried to pick up the bill, but Lia shot him down by laying cash for her meal on the table. "It's okay. Today is normally the day I go out to dinner with Avery." She smiled. "She owes me since she stood me up at the Valentine's Day gala. She had a good reason, though."

"*She* was the person you needed to meet."

The huge wave of relief he felt shocked

him. It shouldn't matter. At all. Unless he wasn't really over her.

He was. He'd spent the last three years doing everything he could to forget her. And while he hadn't completely banished her from his head, he'd at least trapped her in a small corner closet toward the back of his brain.

Seeing her again hadn't released her from that dark room. Had it?

Hell, he hoped not. But at least he understood her reasons for breaking up with him a little more.

"Yep, but she decided to spend time with her romantic interest instead."

"The guy with the guitar?"

"One and the same." She laughed. "Avery swore it would never happen. Swore she was immune. I told her to never say never."

Well, he was pretty sure he could say "never" to his being involved with her again. Once was more than enough.

"I definitely saw something between them when I watched them interact."

Her smile was still there. And this time it was very real. It made something heat inside him.

"Something is an understatement. Carter's the one."

The one. Was there such a thing?

If so, Micah hadn't been it. At least not for Lia.

They made their way out to her car, and his brooding thoughts vanished, a smile taking their place when he spotted her vehicle. It was a little compact model that fit her to a T.

Lia had never been a flashy person, unlike his parents. It was probably one of the things that had attracted him to her. Her dad was a pretty well-known scientist in his own right, and yet she never acted like she'd grown up in an upper-middle-class family—one that had done what a lot of families would have been afraid to do: move here from another country.

Her Italian sometimes still came out when she said certain words or when she got nervous or angry. Her breakup speech had been riddled with little language blips that he was sure came from her background, although he hadn't thought they were cute that time. But looking back, he realized those slip-ups proved that what they'd had hadn't been unimportant to her. Otherwise, she would have sailed through that "I don't think we're meant to be together" speech without a problem. It made the blow that much harder knowing that while she cared about him, it hadn't been enough to make her fight for them. Fight for their future.

Because she hadn't thought they had one.

He crunched himself back into the front seat of her car.

"Micah, seriously, push the seat back. You look ridiculous."

On the ride to the wings joint, it hadn't seemed that important, since he hadn't thought he was going to be in the car for the next couple of hours. But with his knees literally pressed against the console in front of him, every pothole was going to bang them up pretty good.

So this time, he reached down for the lever and pushed the seat back as far as it would go. There. At least if they were in an accident, his legs wouldn't be pushed through his chin.

"Less ridiculous?"

"Much." She took out her phone. "So where to? Any preferences as to car dealerships?"

"Maybe one in this area of town and one over in Metro Center?" He pulled up a map of neighborhoods on his phone. "There's also Music Row, which might be a good location for flyers. I'm trying to think of areas that would get the word out the fastest."

"Okay, how about if we do two car dealerships in the downtown area, since they're closer, and then drive out to the other two spots if it's not too dark. I'm assuming we'll have to make more than one trip. Saint Dolly's is going to call other area hospitals and alert them to what's going on here. Hopefully it's confined to just this one area."

"We can hope." Kind of like his problems with Lia had been confined to one area of his heart. Fortunately he'd contained them in time to keep it from really affecting his life.

When Lia put her turn signal on and headed toward the congested area of downtown, he turned his mind toward helping her navigate and away from everything else.

There had been something heartwarming about seeing Micah scrunched in her passenger seat on the way to the wings joint, but after the strange intimacy that had wrapped around that meal with discussions about their past, she had been loath to carry that intimacy outside the restaurant. So she was glad when he'd pushed his seat back and made the car's interior seem a little less cramped.

Or did it?

The way he'd said he'd met lots of people in Ghana had thrown her for a few seconds. Female people? Or was he just trying to get out of answering what was a rather pointed question? But hadn't his question about their breakup been just as pointed?

She forced her attention to something less personal.

"There are a couple of dealerships off I-40. Do you have a preference of car type?"

He sent her a smile. "Just something a little bigger than a lunchbox."

"A lunchbox?" She laughed, glad things seemed to be heading in a more lighthearted direction. "Are you dissing the big blueberry?"

"Isn't *big* blueberry an oxymoron? There is nothing big in this car."

She looked over at him and raised her brows. "Except maybe its passenger's—"

"Uh-uh-uh. My...er...noggin isn't that big."

She had to hand it to the man. He knew how to make her laugh. And how to leave himself open for the perfect comebacks. "Who said I was talking about your head?"

As soon as the words were out of her mouth, her face sizzled with heat. Okay, so she hadn't been specifically talking about any male parts, although she was pretty sure he was going to take it that way. And maybe her subconscious had thrown that out just to torture her.

Micah didn't reply, although out of the corner of her eye she could see a muscle pulsing in his cheek. In anger? Mirth? Disbelief?

Ha! Well, she had a mixture of all three of those reactions going on herself. But she needed to pull herself together or she was going to do something she regretted. Like wish she was kissing him?

Yes. Exactly like that. Even letting that thought go through her mind had her remembering what it had been like to have the man lock lips with her. And a whole lot more.

Fortunately, they weren't far from the first car dealership.

Five minutes later they were getting out of the car and talking to one of the salespeople. Micah told the man what he was looking for. The salesman glanced at Lia. "Will your wife be driving it a lot?"

"She is not my wife."

He punched those words out in a way that made Lia's eyes widen. It was as if that idea were so far out of the realm of possibility as to be laughable. Only he hadn't laughed. Or even chuckled.

"Sorry. I just assumed…" The man didn't finish that statement. Instead, he dived into a rundown of vehicles that fit Micah's needs.

Lia's mood took a turn for the worse. Maybe she should have let him come on his own.

It didn't take long for Micah to find what he was looking for—an SUV that looked like it would work equally well in town or in the country. "Do you want to take it for a test drive?"

"No, I drove something similar in Ghana, so I'm pretty sure I know what it feels like."

Ah, now that made sense. He would have needed something rugged if he had to travel long distances or over difficult terrain. Her blueberry wouldn't have stood a chance there.

And neither would she, probably. At least not without revealing a lot more about herself than she'd wanted to. Thankfully she'd never had to explain her reasons for not wanting to go, other than what she'd said at Maurio's.

The thought of stepping out of her known world and landing in a place where she'd have to start from scratch? Learn how to tell a whole new load of people apart? No. It would be like moving the furniture in her house around and then trying to somehow make her way through it in the dark. She might not be physically blind, but face blindness still took away one of the principal means of navigating through the world... through relationships. Not recognizing Micah at the benefit was proof of how hard it was.

Dio, she'd experienced enough angst over that to last a lifetime. Besides, her father's reflections on the difficulties her uncle had faced had struck deep...and stayed there. Would knowing about her prosopagnosia have affected her job prospects? She'd like to think not, but in the real world...

She just wasn't willing to take that chance. And right now, she was glad that she'd kept the truth to herself.

As she wandered through the lot, deep in thought about the decisions she'd made in life, Micah went in to seal the deal. Fifteen minutes later, he reemerged.

"Done already?"

"Yep. It'll be delivered to the hotel tomorrow. Unfortunately that means you're stuck with me for the rest of the day. Sorry."

"It's okay. I figured it'd be easier if we're together."

Together. But only in the most superficial of ways. She'd make sure of that.

"Speaking of which, the owner of the dealership said he's willing to put a flyer up inside the building where anyone who visits will see it."

She hadn't really thought about businesses putting them up, but it made a lot of sense. "That's great. I guess we'll have to figure out what we want on them pretty quickly." Which probably meant there were more meetings in the near future if they wanted to get out ahead of this thing. And Lia wasn't sure how she felt about them huddling over pages of ideas.

They got back into the car and started toward the main area of downtown Nashville. "What about one of the parks?"

"We'll need something a little more durable than plain paper if we put them up outside."

She'd thought of that as well. "Maybe a material like the plastic yard sale signs we see around. I'm sure the hospital would let us have some of them printed up."

A couple of miles ahead, they found a park that had a lot of foot traffic. Was it muscle memory that had brought her this way? She swallowed back that thought. Of course not. They had history in a lot of places in Nashville. She found a place to park the car and looked at the green space, her hand hovering over the key in the ignition, hesitating to turn the car off.

As if reading her thoughts, he murmured, "We used to come here to get away from things. I even remember playing hooky on our classes one day."

She remembered that well. She'd been a wreck after a particularly difficult day, and Micah had talked her into taking a walk to clear her head.

Except it hadn't been the walk that had done that. It had been his kiss. A kiss that had turned into two, and then three. And they'd had their first lovemaking session in a secluded area under the cover of trees and shrubbery. They'd both missed their next class. And she hadn't regretted it. She still didn't. She shivered at the memory.

"Yes, we did." She cleared her throat. "I remember this place being pretty busy, which is why I think it might be a good place."

"For flyers?" His smooth words made her

insides quiver. What else had he thought she meant?

"Yes."

"Do you want to get out and look?"

Did she? Would it cause her to relive memories that should be left in their final resting place? But to balk now would be to confirm that she hadn't gotten over him. Or this place. "I suppose we should."

She turned off the car and tossed the keys into her purse. "Maybe we should take a few pictures of likely spots, so we can remember them later."

"Pictures. Now that's a novel idea."

Was he making a joke about their history in this park? Or was he simply taking her words the way she'd meant them? Actually, she didn't really know how she meant anything right now.

They entered the park, and as soon as they did, she saw everything through the eyes of her past. The greenery that beckoned to hikers and runners alike. The cleared areas that appealed to urbanites who liked the solid feel of concrete beneath their feet. And the small stands of trees that were crafted like mini oases. Those had appealed to Micah and Lia on a day when her stress had been decidedly relieved in his arms.

What were they doing here? This was a huge mistake. She was just about to suggest they turn around and go back to the car when she realized they were...there.

Her shaky legs were thankful for the bench that stood just across the pathway from the dense shade of bushes in front of them. She sank onto it, trying to make it seem as natural as possible. She pointed up at the lamppost. "This is one of the main footpaths through the park. We could put a flyer up there." To keep her mind on the task at hand, she aimed her phone at the area and took a picture of it.

Micah sat down next to her. "Do you know where we are?"

Pretend you don't. Act like this is the first time you've ever seen it.

Like when she'd seen him at the gala? Only that hadn't been pretense. She really hadn't known who he was. At first.

But now she did. Her eyes shut. *Dio...* now she did.

"Yes." The word came out a little shakier than she would have liked, but that couldn't be helped. She covered with her next words. "We're at Butler Park. I think it will be an ideal place to advertise. We'll have to get permission from the parks department, of course, and then we'll need to design the flyers and figure out how to mount them and protect them from the—"

"Lia." His voice stopped the manic tumble of words that she'd used to keep the pull of this place at bay. It hadn't worked. Because as soon as he said her name, voices from the past came whispering toward her, sliding past her cheek, her ears, familiar scents filling her nostrils.

She half turned toward him, her words suddenly deserting her. All she could do was look at him. Those gray eyes, that short beard that was unsuccessful in hiding a strong chin and square jaw. These were things that she recognized. That helped her differentiate him from a million other people on this planet. That and the way he made her feel.

Both in the past. And right now. Right here.

"Yes?"

"Do you know *where* we are? Do you remember this very spot in this very park?"

He wasn't going to let her sidestep his original question.

This time her "yes" was whispered, and she didn't try to add anything else to it.

Warm fingers slid down her jaw until he

reached the point of her chin. He cupped it, tipping her face up to his. "This is where it really began."

Yes, it was. The place where sex among the trees had transformed from a mere release of energy into a relationship that not only released energy but gained it back as they shared with each other.

Suddenly she knew he felt it as much as she did. That the magic this park had woven back then was just as potent today as it had been when they were young medical students.

That's when she knew. Knew that she wasn't getting out of this park without getting what she came for. What she longed for.

And that was his kiss.

A small smile played at the corner of his mouth, denting his cheek and making her lean closer to him. Until at last she felt a completely different kind of magic: one where his lips finally touched hers.

CHAPTER FIVE

HE HADN'T MEANT to kiss Lia. But when she sat down on the bench in front of their spot, and he looked into the bushes and saw in his mind's eye their two bodies twined together in an impossible embrace, he hadn't been able to resist saying her name. And when she turned toward him, lips parted, he'd realized he wasn't going to be able to resist her now any more than he'd resisted her all those years ago.

His mouth covered hers, and he sensed more than felt her melt into his embrace. His arms came up and wrapped around her, pulling her closer, her breasts pressed tight against him.

Hell, it had been far too long since he'd held her or any other woman like this. And that was probably why his tongue edged forward and traced her lips with a question.

One that she instantly answered by opening her mouth.

He groaned low in his throat, one hand sliding into the hair at the back of her head and holding her in place as he deepened the kiss. His senses were ignited as memories came at him in snatches, like a set of fireworks that lit the sky for a few seconds before dimming and allowing the next explosion to take its place, each burst more brilliantly colored than the last.

Her fingers gripped his shoulders, clenching and releasing in time with the stroke of his tongue. Just like she'd done hundreds of other times when they'd…

Something between them vibrated. Something that wasn't part of his body.

It happened again, and it took him a few seconds to realize it was someone's phone. Lia's, since his ringer was on.

She jerked back from him, eyes coming up to catch his as she struggled to catch her breath. "What…?"

Damn. He had no idea why he'd just done what he had.

Maybe proving to himself that she'd been as into his touch as he'd been into hers? Had he needed…closure?

As quickly the word popped into his

head, he threw it away. Because that kiss had closed nothing. Instead it had ripped wide-open a door from the past, allowing everything he'd stuffed behind it to come tumbling out.

He quickly forced a smile to his lips to cover his musings.

"Saved by a little vibrator."

Wait. That wasn't the right expression. But the burn of red in her face made the mistake worth it. And it helped him realize she'd been just as caught up in the moment as he had.

The buzzing stopped and then started back up almost immediately. Lia fished her phone out of the pocket of her light jacket and glanced at the readout before frowning. "It's Avery."

She pushed a button, then pressed the phone to her ear. "Hi, Ave, what's up?"

Listening for a second, her frown deepened. "About fifteen minutes, why? We had a pertussis case and were looking at spots to—"

She licked her lips. "Um… I'm with Micah."

Evidently she was warning her friend that she couldn't speak freely. Why? Was she planning on sharing all about that unplanned kiss later on? Would she sit there and dissect it with Avery later on?

"Who?" She listened before exclaiming, "Oh, no! Okay, I'm on my way right now. Get her on the list for one of the OR rooms. The sooner the better. 'Bye."

She looked at him. "Sorry, but I have to cut this field trip short. I'm needed back at the hospital. Can I drop you off somewhere?"

"I can just catch the shuttle at the hospital." Field trip? Really? That kiss was more than just a damned field trip. "Anything I can help with?"

"Avery has been treating one of her patients for some vascular issues in her legs. Well, she'd also started complaining about abdominal pains and just showed up in the ER complaining of severe pain in her belly."

"Vascular issues. Could it be an aneurysm?"

"That's what I'm thinking, or aortic dissection, both of which are medical emergencies."

Micah stood and held his hand out to her. "Let's go, then."

They rushed back to the car, and when Lia's hands were shaking so hard she could barely get the key into the ignition, he took the key from her. "Trade places with me."

"Thanks." The look of relief she threw at him screwed with his insides. But he managed to get out of the car and walk around to the driver's seat. He adjusted the seat and started the vehicle.

Then he turned the car around and aimed it in the direction of the hospital.

Lia couldn't believe she'd let him kiss her. Let? *Dio*, if she remembered right, it had been her who'd leaned toward him and not the other way around. But none of that mattered right now. The fear in Avery's voice had been very real. She remembered her friend asking her if Bonnie had contacted her, and she'd said no. Avery said she was going to get her former music teacher to come in and meet her, but evidently that had all changed. It was now an emergency situation. If it was an aortic dissection—where a weakness in the aorta let blood leak between the layers of the vessel—then time was of the essence, because if it ruptured completely, death could occur within minutes. It sounded like it was down low in the abdominal section of the artery rather than up near the heart. She hoped there was a surgeon at the hospital who could scrub in before she got there, because the longer the wait… It was what killed people before they even realized they were truly sick. She could think of actors and dignitaries alike who had been affected.

"Hurry."

"I'm going as fast as I safely can."

It felt like they were crawling, although when she glanced at the speedometer, they were nearing seventy miles per hour. She was a mess, and even though she was worried about Avery's friend, Lia knew that was only part of the reason for her panic.

Her former lover had kissed her again as if nothing had gone wrong between them. And that scared the hell out of her. How could she have let this happen? Micah deserved better than this. And hell if she hadn't tried to give it to him by breaking things off. Once this was over, she was going to have to make sure he knew that nothing had changed. They were not—nor could they ever—getting back together.

He glanced at her. "You okay?"

Really? He was leading with that?

"Sure. Just fine."

"Stop it, Lia." His hands gripped her steering wheel so hard she was surprised he didn't rip it from the console. "Look, I know that kiss was a mistake. Don't read more into it than there was."

What on earth was that supposed to mean? "I'm not!"

"That's not what I'm seeing by the whole 'ready to run and run hard' vibe you've got going on. Look. It was where we had sex for the first time. It's not surprising that we kissed. Exes get caught in that kind of situation all the time."

They did? And just how did he know that?

I met lots *of people there.* His words from earlier whispered through her skull, pulling pieces of brain matter apart and turning them against each other.

The fact that he'd used the words *had sex* rather than *made love* somehow made what they'd had look cheap and dirty, as if it was just two people with biological urges they'd chosen not to resist.

That hurt worse than the thought of him sleeping with hundreds of other women. But she wasn't about to let him see the truth.

"Sure. Whatever. Just as long as you know it's not going to lead to us having sex again anytime soon."

If she thought she'd shot a well-aimed

arrow and hit a spot it might hurt, she was wrong.

"I never thought it was." He shot her a look. "Did you?"

Actually? If he had kept kissing her like that, they might very well have wound up in that same stand of trees doing the same thing they'd done years ago. And dammit, it wouldn't have been *having sex*, either. They would have been making love. At least it would have been for her.

They made it to the hospital in record time, and when he pulled up in front of the emergency room entrance, she leaped out of the car without stopping to say anything to him and headed through the doors. She'd deal with her keys and the whole car thing later on. Once she found out what was going on with Avery's friend. She had an emergency to see to, one that provided an escape that she welcomed more than she could say.

Avery waved to her from behind the double doors that led to the exam rooms.

"Ultrasound?"

"Yes. Looks like it's an aneurysm in her abdomen. Superior mesenteric. She's trying to act like it's nothing, but it's definitely something."

"Thank God." Even as she said the words,

she knew how they sounded. An aneurysm could be as big an emergency as a dissection if it burst. But depending on how large the bulge was and how weak the vessel walls were, it could buy them more time. "I thought for sure you were going to say she had an aortic dissection. How big is it?"

"Looks fairly large to me. She's had severe varicose veins in her legs, but like I said, she called me complaining of some kind of twinge in her stomach, and I was afraid something else was going on. I wish she had called you like I asked."

"Me, too. Where is she? I'll want to see the location on the ultrasound and determine the size for myself."

Avery led her toward the back, where the exam rooms were. Before she even got there, she heard singing. Two voices were crooning about falling into some kind of fire pit? No, a fiery ring. She shot a glance at Avery, who just shrugged. "I told you. She's trying to pretend nothing is wrong."

Lia could relate to that. She'd been trying to pretend nothing was wrong for most of her life. Doing her best to hide her condition from friends, family...and from the few men she'd had in her life, including Micah. In the end, her secret had cost her that relationship. So she was going to make sure this patient didn't ruin her life doing the same thing she'd done: keeping secrets.

Avery squeezed her arm. "Brace yourself. Her companion is a Johnny Cash impersonator named Levi. In case they ask if you recognize who he is."

"Seriously? Johnny Cash?"

"Yep. Right down to the scar on his chin."

She stopped outside the door where the a cappella voices originated and then pushed through it into the room. Nothing stopped—the music continued, the room's two occupants seemingly oblivious to everything around them. On the exam table was her patient, and her singing partner was…okay, Johnny Cash, just like Avery had said.

The face meant nothing, but the pompadour was there, as were the dark sideburns, craggy line in his cheek and that scar. And he was dressed all in black.

The song lyrics suddenly made sense.

She waited until they were done with the chorus before moving forward, shifting her attention away from the Johnny lookalike and focusing them on her patient.

Bonnie was in a skirt that was pushed up enough to reveal knee-high compression stockings, one of which was up and the other rolled down to her ankle. She looked again at Avery with a question. Avery shook her head to indicate she hadn't done that.

"Hi, Ms. Chisholm, I'm Iliana Costa. You were supposed to call me?"

The woman's lips compressed, and she sucked down an exasperated sigh. "You're Avery's friend."

"I am. I hear you're having stomach pains?"

"They're not bad right now. Just a twinge here and there. I think they're going away, actually." Even as she said it, her face contorted for several seconds before the pain released her.

"Can you show me where it hurts?" she asked Bonnie, not bothering with the pain scale, since it was pretty obvious she was going to underplay her symptoms and her discomfort.

Bonnie ignored the request, saying instead, "I didn't even want to come to the hospital, but Levi here insisted."

"He was right. And Levi is...?"

"He's a Johnny Cash impersonator."

A laugh bubbled up inside her that she had to disguise with a cough. "I gathered that. But who is he to you?"

"He's my...er, sidekick."

Avery shot her a look that said everything. "So it's okay that he's here, I take it."

"Definitely."

Lia nodded. "Good. So where is this twinge, exactly?"

Bonnie pressed her hand on an area in her abdomen.

She looked at her friend again. "Did you save images of the ultrasound?"

"Yep, here they are." She went through the images on the computer in the room. It looked like it was indeed in a section of the mesenteric artery, and the aneurysm had ballooned to about two centimeters. It was a pretty good size. A stent wasn't going to work here. They were going to have to bypass the damaged section, hopefully before it blew out.

She went up to the head of the bed. "Okay, Bonnie, did Avery explain that you have an aneurysm and what that means?"

"She said I probably need surgery. Is that really necessary? It's really not as bad as it was. Can't I just wear a girdle to hold it in, like I do these stocking things?"

Avery stepped forward. "No, because this is deep inside you. If it ruptures, you could very well bleed to death. This is serious,

Bonnie. You can't sing it away. You need to listen to Dr. Costa and get it fixed."

The man at her side moved to the head of the bed, his cologne rolling over Lia in waves. "You're the June to my Johnny. Without you, I'm lost. I need you here."

Lia blinked. As odd as this couple might look together, the concern in the man's voice sounded genuine. He cared about her. "Avery is right. We do need to operate. But once we're finished, you should recover well, as long as you're willing to make some lifestyle changes, starting with your blood pressure."

"I'm a singer. It's a high-stress profession."

"High stress can lead to high blood pressure. But I think we can help you with that with medication, so you'll be able to keep singing."

"Ugh. What do you think Avery? Do I really need to start popping pills? I don't want to be a drug addict like some of those rock stars are."

Her friend smiled. "It isn't exactly 'popping pills.' And it's what I've already suggested. More than once."

Bonnie's lips became a sideways slash that revealed her displeasure, but it didn't completely rule out what they were saying. She reached for her companion's hand. "What do you think, Sugar Lips?"

"I think you need to do what they say. You've known Avery a long time. She won't steer you wrong."

His voice was gravelly and low, and Lia couldn't quite tell if it was his real voice or if he was still playing a part. Whichever it was, he was saying all the right things.

Bonnie closed her eyes and nodded. "When does this surgery thing need to happen?"

The next part was touchy. Avery had told her that Bonnie hated hospitals. She didn't want to scare her off when they were this close to getting her to agree to a much-needed procedure. "It should be done right away. You're experiencing symptoms, which means the aneurysm could be very close to bursting."

"Like it could burst inside me right now?"

"Yes. I'm here now, so let's get this done and behind you."

Avery touched her arm, a question on her face.

Lia motioned toward the door. "We'll be right back. We're going to discuss strategy for a moment."

When Levi nodded, the friends exited to the hallway.

Avery pulled her a little way down the hallway.

"What's going on?" Lia said.

"You look exhausted. Are you sure you're up for this? And was that Mr. Slash and Burn that I saw bringing you in?"

"Would you please stop calling him that?"

"No." Avery laughed. "Because I swear right now you're about to do a 'burn, baby, burn.'" Her friend sang those three words, drawing the last syllable out on a crazy combination of musical notes, her hips swishing in time with each change in pitch.

Her antics caused Lia to make a sound that was halfway between a laugh and a screech. "I am not!"

"You should see your face. And I know what it feels like, because I get that way every time Carter gives me a sideways look."

Lia rolled her eyes. "First of all, that is you being caught up in a love mist and wishing happy endings on everyone around you. Micah and I were over a long time ago."

"Sure, sure. We'll circle back to that. Which brings me to the other subject I mentioned. You look exhausted. I can call someone else in."

"No. She needs the surgery, and I'm already here. There's no reason to call another surgeon. As for the circling back, please don't. I took him to look for a car and to scout out places to hang some posters for the hospital."

"And that wasn't a problem at all?" Her friend studied her face. "Being in the same vehicle with him?"

"Not a problem. At all. At least I hope not." Even as she said it, Micah appeared at the end of the hallway, giving her a quick smile.

Her face turned to lava.

"Slash. And. Burn. Right on cue." Avery bumped her with her shoulder.

Micah reached them and said, "I thought you might be back here. I brought the keys to your car. I parked it in the physicians' lot."

Lia gulped, praying Avery wasn't going to say anything else about Micah's cheek, which was still dented from his smile. "Thanks. You won't have a problem getting back to the hotel?"

"Nope. Can we meet up tomorrow to discuss the situation?"

Avery's head twisted sideways to stare at her, brows raised almost to the ceiling. "There's a situation?"

Dio, was there ever. But it wasn't one she wanted to admit to herself, much less to Avery, especially since her friend was right about her reaction to his smile. It had always been that way. Maybe she would confess to her friend at some point about what had happened in the park, but not until she'd had a chance to analyze it for herself. So she quickly broke down the only situation she wanted to talk about: Sassy and the threat of a pertussis outbreak. She ended it with, "But right now I want to focus on Ms. Chisholm's aneurysm. Any other problem can wait until later."

She said that last part with enough emphasis to hopefully convince Avery—and herself—that it was true. Although she wasn't so sure her brain registered her words. It was already taking chunks of what had happened at the park and blowing them all out of proportion.

Micah glanced at her, and the groove in his cheek kicked back up, causing her to sizzle all over again. He was on to her. Maybe she'd be telling Avery about the park incident sooner rather than later. Because her friend might come up with a worse nickname than Slash and Burn, given enough time.

"Here you go." He reached in his pocket,

and the tinkle of her key ring with its little bell sounded. "What's this, by the way?" He fingered the silver jingle bell attached to the key ring.

"That's Samantha's."

His head tilted. "Samantha's?"

"Her cat," Avery said. "Named for her witchy ways."

"Witchy…"

Lia explained, "She's named after a TV show character. She can be a little temperamental. And she's been known to vanish and reappear at a moment's notice."

The indent in Micah's cheek became a full-blown grin, and she couldn't help smiling back like an idiot. "I take it the bell is to let you know where she is. If that's the case, shouldn't it be with her rather than with you?"

"She…um…somehow got it off her collar."

"Well, I guess that means she knows where you are rather than the other way around. Clever kitty."

The low words made her shiver.

"I hadn't thought about that." She'd just put the bell on her key chain so she wouldn't lose it. Although with how smart Sam was, she wouldn't put it past the cat to have turned the tables on her.

She held her hand out for the keys. "I'm planning on putting it back on her safety collar tonight." The words came out a little more waspishly than she meant them to. "And I'd better get back to my patient if I'm going to get this surgery on the road."

"Anything I can help with?"

"No. But thanks for asking."

He looked dubious but didn't argue. "All right. I'll see you later, then. And I'll be in touch with you about tomorrow."

"Sounds good." She'd worry about tomorrow when tomorrow came.

Thankfully, Avery didn't say anything else as they returned to her patient's room. Lia patted the woman on the hand. "I'm going to make sure we're set as far as an operating room goes. I'll be back in a few minutes to give you an update and explain exactly what our plan is."

Bonnie's surgery was off to a rocky start. The second Lia opened her up, the weakened vessel burst, filling the surgical site with a rush of blood. "I need suction!"

"Stats are dropping, Doctor."

She needed to find that vessel. Lia reached

in with gloved fingers, feeling around as another nurse continued suctioning the area. There!

"Found it. Clamp."

A clamp magically appeared in her hand, and she somehow managed to get it around the upper portion of the injured artery. When they'd suctioned out the rest of the blood, Lia looked at the screens displaying the patient's vital signs. "Okay, she's stable for now. Let's work fast."

This was not how she'd wanted this to go. If the aneurysm was caused by an infection in the vessel, it could have just released a flood of bacteria into her abdomen. What she'd seen on the scans hadn't looked mycotic, but she would rather have clamped the vessel and bypassed it than have it rupture. She could do an intracavity lavage with antibiotics, but there were mixed reviews on whether it actually helped prevent sepsis or not. What she could do instead was start her on a course of IV antibiotics to ward off infection, just in case. "Is the graft ready?"

Another doctor had been busy retrieving a vein from Bonnie's leg to use to replace the part of the damaged artery. "Yes, although I had a heck of a time finding something decent. Just suturing the site closed."

Lia took the section of vessel and used it to resection the two cleaned-up ends of the vessel. Ten minutes later, it was attached. Looking through her loupes, she checked the suture line, making sure the stitches were close and even. "Let's take the clamp off and see what we've got."

The clamp was removed, and they waited. No leaks. Everything looked well sealed. "Send the removed portion to pathology and have them look for signs of infection. I want to make sure we cover all our bases." She gave a relieved sigh and glanced up at the viewing window, where Avery was watching, and nodded to her. Then she turned back to her team. "Let's get her closed up."

An hour later, Bonnie was in recovery, and they'd allowed Levi to join her. She met Avery in the hallway to give her an update. "I want to keep her for a day or two to give her a chance to recover and so we can monitor for signs of infection." She smiled. "And you might see about getting her a private room, in case she wants to put on another concert."

"I'll work on that."

Hopefully she would have the path results back soon and they'd be in the clear. In the meantime, she gave Avery a hug.

She glanced at her phone and saw it was already after nine in the evening. "I think I'm headed home to crash, unless you need me for something else."

"No. Go. I'm going to head home to Carter in a few minutes, too, before he sends out a search party." Her friend smiled. "And thank you for saving her. She's a special lady."

"I can see that. And it was a group effort. But she is going to need to work on her blood pressure."

"I agree. We'll have another discussion about that. Thanks again."

"You're welcome. We need to set up that guac date." She felt for her keys and found them in her pocket. Hopefully he had made it home. "And please, please don't call Micah by that name again."

"Yes, to the guac. On the other thing… I'm not sure. You'll need to convince me that it's no longer an accurate representation. I could call him Mr. Slash and you Ms. Burn, if you'd prefer."

"No. I don't prefer."

Maybe because it was a little close to the truth. She needed to figure out if anyone else could see what Avery evidently could. And, if so, what she needed to do to change it.

CHAPTER SIX

MICAH SPOTTED LIA and Avery the second they came in.

"Damn." The word slipped out before he could stop it.

The elegantly dressed woman seated across from him tilted her head and frowned. "What is it, honey?"

Honey. It was how she'd always referred to him, but he wasn't sure it meant any more now than it had in the past. In fact, the word itself grated on him whenever he heard it on television or between lovers on the street. Because it brought up a whole host of memories he'd rather forget. In fact, he wouldn't be here at all with her if she hadn't contacted him and asked if they could meet.

He shook himself from his thoughts. "Nothing. I was just thinking of something."

Lia had needed to attend to another emergency surgery two nights ago when they were supposed to meet up about the vaccination campaign. And he actually hadn't seen her since then, since he'd been busy as well. Sassy was still in the hospital. So far no other pertussis cases had come in, but it was still early, and adults tended to fend off the illness better than infants. Sassy had been touch and go, but today, for the first time, it seemed she might be improving.

Something he wasn't sure if Lia knew. He probably should tell her.

While Lia looked straight ahead as if she didn't care who was here, Avery's gaze scanned the faces in the room. Her glance collided with his, and she smiled, then jabbed Lia with her elbow. Great. He'd been hoping he wouldn't actually see anyone he knew here.

The woman leaned close to Lia and whispered something. Lia stopped in her tracks, and her eyes slowly swung in his direction. Okay, well, it looked like he wasn't getting out of here unscathed. He gave her a half smile. Lia's teeth came down on her lower lip, rubbing along it in a move he found fascinating. Why had she done that? Not that he minded.

Actually he thought it was pretty damned…

Inconvenient. That's the word he was looking for.

"Are those friends of yours?" His attention swung back to his companion.

Oh, hell. The last thing he wanted to do was to introduce her to Avery and Lia. Especially since Lia had never met her. Not even when they were dating. Although maybe it had been a sign of things to come.

He struggled to find a way to describe Lia. "They work at the same hospital as I do."

Just then, the pair's trajectory changed, and they headed toward Micah's table, Lia hanging back and looking like this was the last place she wanted to go. Her first reaction to seeing him might have been crazy sexy, but right now she looked pretty miserable. But at least she'd recognized him this time.

Then they were standing in front of them, and he had a decision to make. So he stood and forced a smile that wasn't real this time. "Hi, ladies. I didn't know you liked this place."

"Best guacamole in the state. It's where we always come," Avery said with a touch of pride in her voice.

He remembered asking Lia for a recommendation of that very dish, and this wasn't the place she'd named. He looked at her. "Is it now?"

Her teeth slammed down on her lip again, and this time a flush leached into her cheeks. "It's only one of the places I eat guacamole."

Avery's head swung around. "*One* of them? I thought you said Gantry's guac was a cut above any other restaurant's? Not that I disagree. It's fab."

So Lia hadn't wanted to bring him here. Why? Did she consider him some kind of infectious disease that would contaminate this place and ruin it for her?

Maybe it was part of the same reason she'd broken up with him. He hadn't bought the whole "We want different things from life" crap she'd thrown at him after graduation. Something had happened. Something that had changed the way she saw him in a nanosecond. But he couldn't force her to tell him if she didn't want to. And he'd been so shocked and hurt that he'd just wheeled away from her and gotten the hell out of there. He'd wound up in a bar very much like this one.

And after all this time, he wasn't going to sit here and second-guess every single thing he'd said or done. Not like he had back then.

"And who is your companion?" Avery gave him a guarded look that he could swear harbored a gleam of disappointment. In what?

He glanced at the woman seated at his table, realizing that through the modern marvels of plastic surgery, she didn't look much older than he did.

Okay, so this was even worse than he'd thought. He did not want Lia thinking he'd kissed her and then immediately gone out and found someone else. Although she probably wouldn't care one way or the other.

"I was just telling her about you both, that we work at the same hospital."

Lia stared down at her feet as if she couldn't bear to look at him. So she'd thought exactly that. That this was his date. That was so far from the truth that it was actually ludicrous.

So with his next words, he allowed a hint of a smile to play across his lips. "Lia and Avery, I'd like you to meet Monica Corday. My mother."

Her head whipped up as shock wheeled through her. This woman was Micah's mom and not his—?

As if summoned, the woman uncoiled

herself from her chair and stood. Out came a perfectly manicured hand on which was some pretty impressive jewelry. "I'm so pleased to meet you both."

Her voice was smooth, with a perfect southern drawl that made Lia's remaining accent feel thick and clumsy. She dreaded opening her mouth.

Avery broke in and saved her the trouble, giving back a greeting gripping the other woman's hand. "Pleased, I'm sure." The cool words held just a touch of prickle that no one but Lia would have sensed. It was as if she'd sensed how unsure Lia felt and was moving in to protect her. Just like her dad always had.

A dangerous prickling occurred behind her eyes. She forced it away with a couple of hard blinks.

She appreciated Avery's efforts, but she could fight her own battles. "It's very nice to meet you, Mrs. Corday, I'm Lia Costa."

Although her condition kept her from seeing the resemblance between mother and son, it didn't stop her from noticing that when Monica Corday smiled, there were very few facial lines activated. Botox. A good deal of it, if she had to hazard a guess. Not like her son, whose smile revealed a wonderful network of lines that made her stomach wobble. And that dimple…

Slash and Burn. Hell if Avery hadn't hit the nail on the head.

The insincere curve of lips appeared again. "Would you two care to join us?"

Dio. When they'd first come in and Avery had pointed him out, she'd thought Micah was here on a date. Outrage had gathered in her chest that she'd done her best to banish. It was none of her business whom he did and didn't go out with. But on the heels of that kiss they'd shared? Really?

To find out this was actually his mom had been even more shocking, if that were possible. Micah had said he and his parents didn't see eye to eye. She was starting to see why. This clinic-crafted person was nothing like the man she used to love.

"Thank you, but no. I'm sure you two have a lot to talk about." Too late she remembered that he'd said his father was ill. So her words sounded terrible.

One of Micah's brows crooked up as he smiled.

How could he smile? His dad was sick. "I, um meant, since you've been gone for so long."

Micah was still standing, and his hand

slid next to hers, pinkie finger barely grazing hers for a second as if to reassure her. "I knew what you meant."

Her throat clogged. He was giving her a pass, even though he probably shouldn't have. This man affected her thought processes in so many ways that it wasn't even funny. He'd always done so, but it was disappointing that he still had this effect on her. She should be well and truly over him by now. But she wasn't. Because she hadn't broken up with him because she'd no longer loved him. She'd broken up with him for just the opposite reason. She loved him so much that she didn't want him saddled with someone who would always have trouble recognizing people she'd known for years. It would be even worse if he'd had to drag her overseas with him.

Even if he didn't find her condition embarrassing, she did. And she didn't want him going through what her dad had had to deal with: stepping in to protect his brother from ridicule. And how many times had her parents had to explain and make excuses for her when she tripped over an identity? The thought of Micah doing that made her cringe.

She looked at Micah's mom and tried to

pick out things about her that she would remember the next time she saw her. Lack of lines. Long blond hair that was the same color as Micah's. A painted-on mole at the corner of her left eye. Except that might not always be there. Maybe she dotted it on periodically and left it off at other times. Lia's eyes went crazily from feature to feature before finding something else. Her nose was slightly crooked, taking a tiny jog to the left. She wondered if it had been broken at some time in the past. Okay. Blond hair. No lines. Crooked nose.

Avery, who hadn't said anything for a minute or two, spoke up. "Lia's right. We have some business to discuss, anyway, so maybe another time."

"Certainly." Monica's response was as smooth as ever, giving no hint that her husband, who wasn't here at the restaurant with them, was ill. Although that probably was why Micah was here—to discuss things. Although maybe not. Maybe they'd already made their amends. Maybe their family was closer than hers now. In the two days since she last saw him? Hardly likely.

And Micah's eyes held a wariness that she didn't like. She might not recognize him by the parts of his face, but she knew him in a way that no one else would. At least that's what she told herself. Who knew if that was actually true or not. Surely his mom knew him well, since she'd been a part of his life since birth.

So she decided to follow Avery's lead and forced a smile she didn't feel. "It was nice meeting you, Mrs. Corday."

"You as well, dear."

She threw one last look at Micah, who nodded. She had no idea what it meant, so she just turned and went in the other direction, following Avery toward a table on the other side of the room.

Lia dropped into her chair with a sigh, holding up two fingers when their usual waitress glanced in their direction. She would know what she meant. They always got margaritas and guacamole with chips when they came here. She turned back to Avery. "Oh, God. That was one of the most uncomfortable experiences ever."

"You mean with Slash and Burn? He didn't look any more comfortable than his dear old mama did."

Needing something to fiddle with, she grabbed a napkin from the table and worried the edge of it. "I had no idea she was his mother. She looks a little young."

"You never met her while you were dating? And the fountain of youth that particular woman drank from comes at a hefty price tag at the hands of a good surgeon."

She had to agree with her. "I'm sure. And no, I never met her. Not once."

"He was probably afraid you'd run away and never come back. I might."

She kind of had run and never come back. But not because of his mother. Because of her own fears. "He said he and his parents didn't see eye to eye. At least that's why he never introduced us, I thought. But who knows? That was a long time ago. So let's not talk about them. Let's talk about your new life with Carter."

It worked. Avery moved the conversation over to something that was near and dear to her heart. And as she talked about the progression that led to their engagement, Lia smiled. "I saw Micah at the Valentine's benefit, and he thought there was some pretty heavy chemistry going on between the two of you."

"There was. But we're not the only ones who have some wild chemistry going on."

So much for keeping things shifted away from her. "If you're talking about me and Micah, that chemistry is old news. There was some at one time, as you know, but not any longer."

"Are you really sure about that, Lia?"

She crooked one shoulder up. "It's what it needs to be." She paused, torn about whether to say anything or not. But she and the ER nurse rarely kept things from each other. Especially when they were at Gantry's for guac and talks. So she plowed forward. "Except...we kissed. And it was... Let's just say I could be in a lot of trouble."

Avery sat back in her chair. "You kissed! When did this happen?"

She did her best to angle her body so Micah couldn't see her face. Or read her lips. "The day of Bonnie's surgery. We were actually in the middle of it when your call came through." Lia had to admit it felt good to get this off her chest.

"Why on earth did you answer the phone?"

"*Dio*, what was I supposed to do? I figured it was something pretty important or you wouldn't be calling me. And actually, it was a blessing. The last thing I needed to be doing was kissing Micah Corday."

"Why?"

She was stunned. "What do you mean, why? Our relationship is over. Finished. *Terminata.* To dredge it up now would be just plain stupid, since I have no intention of getting involved with him again. It was a mistake last time. It would be a mistake this time."

"You never told me exactly what happened between you last time."

Even though her friend knew about her diagnosis, she doubted Avery would agree with her reasons for ending it with Micah.

"I just realized it was never going to work between us. He wanted to go to Africa, and I wanted to stay here. In Nashville."

She prayed Avery wouldn't keep digging.

Her friend sighed, then slid her hand over hers. "I'm sorry. I remember how hard it was for you to get over him. I can't imagine what it must be like to work with him. But that kiss…"

"It was a shock to realize he's going to be staying at the hospital, for sure. I'm hoping it gets easier as time goes on." She sighed. "As for the kiss, I think seeing him again dragged up a lot of old feelings."

"I bet." Her friend glanced over at the other table. "Don't look now, but Mr. Slash and Burn is looking in our direction."

"Avery, seriously. And I'm sure he's just looking around the room. I do hope he and his mom are getting along better, though. Especially with his dad being ill."

"Is it serious?"

"Serious enough to bring him home from Ghana."

Avery's lips twisted. "So that's why he's here. That stinks."

"Yes, it does." Her heart ached for Micah. He'd rarely talked about his parents. So there must be a huge mess of conflicting emotions involved in returning to Nashville.

The waitress set their drinks in front of them, along with two large bowls of guacamole and chips. "Anything else?"

"Not yet," Avery said, "but we may need some more drinks by the time this is all over with."

Debbie, who had waited on them more often than not, gave them a sympathetic smile. "Just send me a signal when you're ready."

"Thanks." Lia waited for the woman to leave and then blew her breath out in a rush. "Why does life have to be so complicated?"

"Tell me about it." Avery smiled. "But sometimes it works out in unexpected ways. Look at me and Carter. Maybe this is another of those times."

Lia was happy for her friend. Happy that

she'd found a person to spend her life with. Happy to see her friend so relaxed and at peace. But things didn't always work out that way. At least not for her and Micah. Even if that kiss had been wildly exciting and crazy good, it was doubtful Micah would ever fully forgive her for dumping him the way she had. And really, nothing had changed. She had the same fears now that she'd had back then. It was why her dating life basically sucked. She didn't see herself settling down and getting married. Having children. Not with the way she was wired.

"It's not, but I'm okay with it." She smiled. "I do hope Bonnie and Levi-slash-Johnny have a happy ending, though."

"They are a wild pair, aren't they? But they really care about each other."

"I'm hoping she'll be released tomorrow or the next day. Did she see you sing at the Valentine's Day benefit?"

Avery nodded. "She did. It was hard getting up there without my sister, but Carter helped me get through it. So did you and Bonnie."

Avery's sister had died of cancer a couple of years ago. It was the main reason her friend had had trouble singing again.

"I think April would be very proud of you, honey."

"I hope so." With that, her friend lifted her glass and said, "Let's toast to new beginnings."

Lia hoped she was talking about her own circumstances and not about her and Micah. Because sometimes there were no new beginnings. Or at least no retreading of old paths. And in this case, she had to believe it was for the best. Even if her heart might disagree.

CHAPTER SEVEN

A KNOCK SOUNDED on the door to Micah's office Monday afternoon. He'd already had a difficult weekend between meeting with his mom and going to see his dad the next day. His dad was a shadow of the strong, commanding man he'd once been. The change had come as a shock and made him realize that though he might not have agreed with the way they'd raised him, he'd been right to come home and try to make peace with the parts of his childhood that had been difficult. That included his parents.

"Come in."

The door opened, and Lia peeked in, a look of uncertainty on her face.

He motioned her inside. "Do you know?"

"Know what?" She slid into the room and perched on one of the chairs in front of his desk, looking like she might like to get up and take flight.

"Sassy, the baby who has pertussis, is being released today."

"That's great," she started, only to stop when he held up his hand.

"It's good that she's better, but there are a couple of reports that other area hospitals have seen some cases over the weekend. One of them is a neighbor of Sassy's family."

Her eyes closed before reopening. "God. I was hoping it was going to be confined to the two families who got together."

"So did I." He picked up a pencil and tapped the eraser end on a map on his desk. "The other cases don't appear to have any ties to the families. But there are always grocery stores or any number of places where a cough can cause an outbreak."

"If this gains speed…"

"I know. Which is why I think we need to prioritize getting some of these posters up. How busy are you today and tomorrow?"

"I have a surgery and a couple of consults to do tomorrow morning, but nothing urgent. I was going to head to the ER after that and pitch in where I could."

"Do you have time to talk about the design? You always did have a flair for putting things like that onto paper."

"Me?" Her voice squeaked in a way that made him smile.

She liked to sketch, and she was good. Micah remembered sitting beside her on the couch while she doodled on a pad. Sometimes the drawings were of things they'd seen that day. Sometimes they were musculature contained within the human body. And sometimes they were things as simple as the fire in the fireplace.

"Yes. You." He hesitated, not sure he should say anything about Thursday night. "It looked like you and Avery had fun at Gantry's."

"We did. Did you and your mom have a productive talk?"

He leaned back in his chair and looked at her. "I don't know about productive. But I think we made a little bit of progress. And I saw my dad."

"How did that go?"

"I'm not quite sure. But we'll see where it leads." He glanced at her. "Let's talk about making a mockup that we can take to Arnie. Can we work on that today?"

"Surely the hospital can hire someone for that part?"

Micah lifted his brows. "I'm sure they can, but all I envision is it taking forever to get all the parties to agree on something. By that time, a few cases could turn into hundreds."

If anyone knew about that, it was him. In Ghana, there hadn't been near the amount of bureaucracy that there was here, and yet it still took forever to get anything accomplished. "If you could sketch a couple cradling a baby with worried expressions on their faces, we can put together a slogan together. The sooner we get this down on paper, the sooner we can hang them around town."

Her features seemed to blanch. "I—I'm not good at drawing faces."

"I've seen some of your drawings, remember? They're really good. We wouldn't need a lot of detail, just kind of neutral features… you could depict worry through their posture, or by how they're huddled together."

She relaxed into her chair. "So just eyes, nose and mouth that could belong to anyone. I wouldn't have to make them distinctly different from each other."

"No." Was it weird that she was hung up on this particular part of the process? Well, maybe drawing faces was harder than it looked. "Just kind of like cartoon characters."

"Cartoon characters." She nodded as if thinking about something. "Actually, that's not a bad idea. If we could make it look like a comic strip, only on a much larger scale, it might attract the attention of adults and children alike."

"I like it." He grabbed a piece of paper and came around to the other side of the desk, sitting in the empty chair and putting the paper between them. "So can we work on it now?"

"You don't have anything else to do?"

"Infectious diseases are what they hired me for, so this needs to top my to-do list."

Her warm scent, probably carried on air currents from the climate control system, drifted over to him, reminding him of that kiss they'd shared. It was heady and made him wonder if having her here in his office with the door closed was such a good idea.

Of course it was. He was an adult. And he would act like it. No mooning over her. No looking for chances to touch her, like he'd done in the past.

Like he'd done at Gantry's?

He reached across her to get to his pencil cup, grabbing two pens and handing her one. Their fingers touched, and a frisson of electricity shot through him. He hadn't tried to touch her that time. It was an accident.

Ignore it. Ask a question. Anything to shift his attention back to the job at hand. "So what are we looking to convey?"

She made a humming sound and touched the top of the pen to her lip, using the pressure to click the mechanism that caused the ball point to emerge.

Micah swallowed, remembering how her teeth had captured that very same lip.

"We want to have a sense of urgency, right? People are getting sick and we want to somehow stop it." Her light brown eyes sought his.

He nodded. "Yes. So how do we do that?"

"Maybe we have a mother with an infant in her arms just as her husband or significant other comes into the room. She's holding the baby close and is looking at the man. We could use a dialogue box to show the baby coughing."

"Would there be actual dialogue between the couple?"

"I don't think so. We have a pretty diverse population here. If we could get the idea across using just the pictures of the cartoon—minimal words—it might be better."

He nodded, trying to think of a way to do

that. "So we could have this couple with a sick baby in the first cartoon slide. The next one could be a hospital scene? With multiple couples holding babies, all of whom have the same 'cough' bubble above them."

"That's good. I like it." She turned a sheet of paper so it was horizontal and divided it into three sections. Quickly she sketched a cartoon couple in the first section, just their bodies and heads, and she actually drew them from the behind, so there were no faces at all in them, but you could clearly tell it was two adults with a baby between them. She penned a dialogue bubble above the infant with "Cough-cough" written in bold, jagged strokes. "How about this?"

It was perfect. There was an element of fear in the adults' posture, the merest hint of a nose on each, as their faces were turned slightly inward to look at each other. He'd known she could do it. "That's just how I envisioned it. Can you do the next one? The hospital scene?"

She touched the pen to her lip, tapping it a couple more times. His senses reacted all over again, remembering the slide of his lips across her mouth. How smooth it was. How warm and moist and...

Shaking himself from the memory, he

forced himself to focus as her pen started scratching in the next box. Three couples were now seated, same perspective, except for one standing adult who faced them. This character wore a lab coat with what was clearly a stethoscope around his neck. The face was a simple oval, devoid of features or emotion. Three dialogue bubbles hovered over the scene this time, each with the same words in them. It was an ominous scene. Outside the hospital windows, there were dark clouds, and she used hash lines to shade the space to make it look gloomy.

"Yes. That's good, Lia. Very good."

When she looked at him this time, there was a sense of relief on her face. Surely she wasn't worried about him rejecting what she'd put on that page. And the fact that she could do it so quickly was exactly what he'd hoped for. "Are you sure?"

"I am. Absolutely." He nudged her with his shoulder. "This is why I didn't want the hospital to farm it out to a business. It would have taken forever. So the last square..."

"I have an idea. How about this?" She quickly drew the same three chairs, empty this time. There was an empty hypodermic needle in the top left corner. The view outside the hospital showed a couple walking down the sidewalk with a stroller—the top of a tiny head peeking out. The scene was idyllic with trees and fluffy clouds. There was a sense of well-being. Peace even. And no dialogue bubbles.

Across the top of the page she wrote,

Whooping cough
A not-so-silent killer
Save a baby's life
Get vaccinated

"We can put the hospital logo and a number for information. Or even for the CDC."

"Yes." He glanced at his watch. "Fifteen minutes. That's all it took. Hell, Lia, you are amazing."

"No. I'm not, really." She turned toward him. "It's not that great."

It was. And so was she. Her beautiful eyes were looking at him in that way she had of skimming quickly over his face before moving beyond it to dwell on other places, studying them intently. It had always made him feel as if she didn't really see him the way other women did: as in his physical appearance. Being valued for such a shallow thing had made him feel almost as invisible as he'd felt as a kid, only in a different way.

Lia had never commented on his face. Except for that line in his cheek, which she'd loved to trail her fingers down.

She'd made him feel seen. Really seen. In a way no one else had.

His hand lying on the desk slid closer to hers before he pulled himself up short. What was he doing? That shared kiss had reminded him of all the things that had been good about their relationship. But when it had imploded...

Yeah. That had been bad. Really bad.

Not a good idea to let himself get drawn back in. He wasn't sure if what she'd said about Ghana was the entire truth or if she had commitment issues or what, but he really didn't want to push replay on whatever had happened at the end. So he did something to drag his attention back where it should be—on the cartoon she'd sketched.

"It is great, and I'm going to prove it to you." He pulled out his cell phone and dialed.

A minute later, Arnie answered.

"Hey, do you have time to look at something? It'll only take a minute."

"Sure. Where are you? Your office?"

"Yep, do you want us to run by with it?"

"Us?"

He glanced at Lia. "Dr. Costa made a mockup for the vaccine campaign we talked about last week."

"Good. That'll save me from having to get a committee together, if it's good. I'll run by your office. I'm on my way out anyway."

"See you in a few minutes, then."

He hung up, only to note that Lia's face was strained. "Are you okay?"

"Are you sure this is good enough to show him?"

"I promise I would have told you if it wasn't."

She looked down. "There aren't any actual faces."

Cocking his head, he looked at the drawing. "You know, I think it's better this way. Those images could represent anyone. Maybe a passerby will mentally superimpose their own image or the likeness of someone they know."

She quickly added a few things to the drawing: a dog on a leash in the last image. A crowd of people outside the window of the first scene, depicting how whooping cough could spread in gatherings.

By the time she was finished, a knock sounded at the door, followed by Arnie coming into the room. He came over to the desk and stood by Lia. "Is this it?"

"Y-yes."

She was nervous. And Lia was rarely nervous. She normally knew her own mind and was confident in her abilities.

Arnie stared down at the picture for a while. Then said, "This is excellent. From one ill child to three, and then along comes the vaccine and empties out the waiting room. I like the touch of showing a happy— and healthy—family walking outside the hospital." He picked it up and went over to the copier and made a duplicate. "I'm going to keep this one, if that's okay. Can you take these to a printer and have them printed, blowing a few into poster-size prints? We'll stamp them with the hospital logo and number and display the large ones here at home and distribute the others to various business. We'll also hang them in places where it's legal to do so."

"I'll need to clean it up a little before we do that," Lia murmured.

"No. I want it left just like this. There's no need to clean anything up. And I know the board will agree with me on this."

Micah smiled at her. "Do you believe me now?"

"I guess so."

Arnie leaned down and took one of the other sheets of paper, scribbling down a name. "This is who the hospital uses for printing materials. Do you think you can get this over there?" He glanced at his watch. "They're open for another hour or so. Order what you need."

"We'll take care of it." Micah glanced at her with raised brows, asking her the question. She answered with a nod.

With that, the hospital administrator opened the door again and thanked them before leaving as quickly as he'd arrived.

"If you can go with me, I actually have my new car, so I can drive this time."

She shrugged. "Well, I guess I don't have a choice, since Arnie made it pretty clear he wants these done immediately. And I do agree with him, it's just…"

"Just what?"

She shook her head. "Nothing. Just wish I had more time to perfect it."

"It'll be okay. You know Arnie better than I do. Would he truly let us print something—something that represents the hospital—if he didn't think it would stand up to scrutiny? I wish I'd had one of your prints in Ghana."

That last statement had slipped out before he could stop it. He'd meant it in a generic way. Right?

Because she'd made it clear back then—and now—that she wasn't interested in him on a personal level.

And that kiss?

He had no idea what that had been about. For her or for him.

Lia glanced over at him. "Thank you." The words were spoken softly with a hint of meaning that he wasn't sure he understood. Or that he wanted to understand.

"If you're ready?" He grabbed a notebook from the back of his credenza. "Let's slide it in here to keep it from getting bent or damaged."

She handed him the drawing, and he tucked it inside the front cover. Then they moved out of the room and headed out of the hospital.

CHAPTER EIGHT

GORDY'S PRINTING WAS busier than she'd expected. There were four people ahead of them, and it was only thirty minutes until their six o'clock closing time. It must be because some folks were coming right after work.

"Did you find a place to live other than the hotel yet?"

"No. Not yet. But then again, it's been so busy I haven't really had a lot of time."

She thought for a second. "I know you and your parents aren't super close, but—"

"No. That wouldn't work."

He shut her down before she'd even finished saying what she'd been going to say. That maybe it would give him time to be with his dad. Especially since he admitted himself that life was extra busy.

As if realizing how short he'd sounded, he touched her hand. "Sorry. I know it would be a good thing, but my mom and dad… I think it would be hard on both sides. I don't want to put my mom in the middle, feeling like she needs to placate both of us. And my dad—well, let's just say he's not the man I remember, and I don't want to stress him out unnecessarily."

"Is he undergoing treatment?" One of the customers left, and the line moved forward.

"He just started. They're hoping for remission."

He'd said *they*. Surely Micah wanted remission for his dad as well.

Another customer slid out of line, going through the door. Okay, so this was moving quicker than she'd thought it would.

"How probable is that?"

"From what my mom said, there's about a thirty percent chance he'll achieve it."

She couldn't stop herself from looping her arm through his and squeezing it before forcing herself to let go. "I know I've said it before, but I'm really sorry. I can't imagine what that has to be like for your family, and since you're their only child, it makes it hard on you as well."

"Well, as their only child, it's why I came home."

Said in a way that let her know that his

return had nothing to do with her. Not that she'd thought it had. She'd just been trying to sympathize with him.

It was their turn, so they moved to the front. Micah opened the notebook and pulled out her sketch. "We need some prints of these. About three poster-size and we need some flyer-size prints as well, but we need them in some kind of heavier paper that's impervious to water."

"We have weatherproof sheets that are about the thickness of cardstock. They're actually plastic, but we can print on them." The clerk was young, with straight dark hair that fell to his shoulders. He looked hip and artsy, a ring on his thumb boasting an ankh symbol. His nails were painted black. A small name tag on his dark polo shirt read Curtis.

He was definitely different from the cowboy types that Nashville was famous for.

"Weatherproof," Micah said. "Sounds like what we need."

The guy took a look at the sketch. "Who drew this?"

"I did." Her heart was in her throat, wondering if he thought it was ridiculous.

He looked up. "I can't accept it like this."

Oh, God. He did think it was ridiculous.

But before she could agree with him, he turned the paper toward her and rummaged through a drawerful of different kinds of pens before finally selecting one. "You really need to sign it. There are people out there who wouldn't think twice about ripping this design off and then claiming it as their own."

"Surely not."

"Hey," said Curtis. "People steal songs and lyrics all the time in this town—you think they wouldn't steal art?"

Art? Was he kidding?

Micah moved close enough to give her hand a squeeze. "Do you believe me now?"

She hadn't. Not really. Until this moment. She looked at her sketch, trying to see what they saw in it. But she just couldn't. She'd always liked to doodle as a kid and had gotten in trouble for doing that in school lots of times.

The young man held out a pen. "Even just your initials with today's date in the bottom right corner will do, but signing your name would be better."

She took the writing instrument and scribbled *L. Costa* along with the year in small letters at the corner of the last scene. "Like this?"

"Yes, perfect." Curtis blew on the lettering for a second or two before finding a plastic sleeve and sliding the drawing inside it. "And I didn't know that whooping cough was making a comeback."

Micah spoke up. "It's always been here. We're just trying to make sure what's out there doesn't turn into an epidemic."

"Good. My wife is actually eight months pregnant." The guy grabbed a pad of paper. "So three posters and how many flyers?"

"Let's go with a hundred."

A hundred of her sketches were going to be floating around Nashville? It made her a little uncomfortable, but if it saved lives...

Curtis scribbled down their order, his ankh ring catching the light a couple of times. "If you ever need a job, we have a design team that would love to have you on it."

She laughed. Okay, well, that was unexpected. "Thank you, but I think I'm better suited to being a doctor."

"If you ever change your mind, let me know." He added up the costs. "Do you have a requisition from the hospital?"

"No," Micah said. "But if you call in the morning and ask to talk to Arnie Goff, he'll give you a number. He's the hospital administrator over at Saint Dolores."

"Ah, Saint Dolly's. I was born there. My wife and I were actually in the nursery at the same time."

Lia's eyes widened. "Well, that's a coincidence."

"We were both preemies, and the hospital has a kind of reunion every year for us. We started dating in high school. Went to prom together."

"I've heard of those reunions. That's wonderful." What a romantic way to meet your future spouse. "Are you planning to have your baby at Saint Dolly's?"

"Yes, but we'll hopefully not wind up in the preemie ward."

"Well, I hope everything goes well for all of you."

"Thanks." He touched the plastic sleeve containing her sketch. "I hope everything goes well with this. And I'll check with our doctor to make sure we don't need a booster."

"That's great." Lia fished in her purse and found one of her cards and scribbled her number on the back. "Let me know if there's anything I can do. I'm not in obstetrics, so definitely check with your doctor, but if you have any questions, please don't hesitate to call." She wasn't sure why she'd done that.

It was rare that she ever gave out her personal cell phone number, but there was just something about the kid she liked. His love for his wife and future baby were obvious.

"Wow, thanks. I will. Jenny is a little nervous about things. This is our first. We got married last year."

Fortunately there was no one else waiting behind them. "Well, the best of luck to both of you."

"Thanks. To you both as well."

Did he think they were a couple? Surely not.

Micah's quick grin said otherwise, making her face heat like molten lava. He slashed, she burned. *Dio*, Avery really was right. "When do you think the printing can be done once you get Mr. Goff's approval?"

"It should be done in a couple of days. So maybe check back on Wednesday?"

"We'll be here." With that, Micah turned away from the desk and headed toward the door.

He'd said *we* as if it were a given that they'd arrive back here together. Lia wasn't so sure that was a good idea. But she'd address that later. If needed, she'd make sure she had something else scheduled. Because being with him today had really rattled her.

Especially when she'd been drawing that sketch, feeling his presence next to her. Feeling his eyes on her as her pen moved over that sheet of paper. It had been unnerving.

And exhilarating. In a way she hadn't felt in a long time. Maybe even since they'd been together.

They walked over to the paid parking garage, Lia pulling her coat around her against the nippy temperatures. Micah showed the attendant their all-day pass as they walked by him. "You know there's free parking not far from here."

"I know, but this was faster, and since I wanted to make it to the shop before it closed, it seemed the best solution. And it's where I used to park when I was in this part of town."

"I remember that from when we were in school."

"Yes, we spent a little bit of time kissing in this garage."

Her face heated yet again. Yes, they had.

They moved into the building and headed toward the back. Even in the paid garage, it had been hard to find a spot, so Lia knew he was right in saying this had been the best option.

They found his car in one of the darker

areas, and Micah pressed the mechanism to unlock the vehicle. Going around to the passenger side, she got in, the scents of leather and Micah surrounding her as she sank into the comfortable seat and clicked her belt.

Dio, it was like days gone by.

Micah got into the driver's seat and started the car, waiting for it to warm up for a minute or so before turning the heat on. She turned her vents toward her.

"Cold?"

"It's a little chilly out there." She glanced at him. "You probably should have worn something heavier."

"I actually enjoy the cold after spending some hot days in Ghana."

"What was it like?" She'd been afraid to go, but that didn't mean she wasn't curious.

"The people were wonderful, but it had its challenges, just like every place." He sat back in his seat and turned his torso to look at her. "Seasons of the year were measured more by dry or rainy rather than temperatures, but it was rare for it to drop below the mid-seventies, and hundred-degree days were not unusual."

A shiver went through her, whether from the thirty-degree weather and wind outside today or from being in a warm car with Micah's low voice washing over her. She could listen to the man forever.

"Wow. Nashville gets hot, but we always know there are cooler days coming. Not sure how I would have handled the constant heat."

"Your body actually adjusts after a while. And when there's so much need around you, it's easier to focus on what's important."

Which made her reasons for not going seem purely selfish.

"I can imagine. How hard was it coming back?"

He gave a half shrug. "I needed to. So I did."

The vehicle was warming up, so Lia allowed herself to relax into the seat. "I hope your father's doctors are able to help him."

"It feels kind of weird to say this, but so do I."

"Weird?"

He frowned. "Weird isn't really the right word. Maybe hypocritical would be better. My mom wrote while I was in Ghana, but... well, there are still some problems between us. So I don't feel I have the right to wish one way or the other."

"What was it you disagreed on?"

"Disagreed?"

Maybe that wasn't the right word. "You said you didn't see eye to eye with them, so I just thought…"

"Ah, I see. It wasn't anything specific. We were just never close."

"Maybe now's the time to change some of that?" Lia had felt awful about not being honest with Micah back then. But she'd honestly believed it was the right thing to do at the time. And she couldn't go back and undo anything that had happened. She couldn't undo the hurt. For either of them.

Maybe that's how Micah felt. Like it wasn't possible to undo anything that had happened with his parents. So why bother trying?

Except Lia did want to make things right with him. Not to have a relationship again— she had killed her chances of that. But maybe she could at least let him know that she was sorry. Sorry for hurting him. Sorry for letting things between them go as far as they had before breaking it off.

She took a deep breath. "Hey. I really am sorry for the way things ended between us. I should have stuck around and talked things through a little more instead of taking off like I did. I just realized at that moment that I couldn't be in a relationship. Not with you.

Not with anyone else. It had nothing to do with you personally. I really did care about you."

"Really?" His eyes hardened. "It was kind of hard to tell that day."

"I know. I thought it was better to make the break quickly, that it would hurt less. And I knew how much you wanted to work with Doctors Without Borders."

"It didn't. Hurt less." A muscle worked in his jaw, and there was no sign of that sexy crease he sported. "I went out and got drunk that night."

A swift pain went through her heart. She'd known she'd hurt him, but to picture him alone in a bar hunched over drink after drink… She reached for his arm, her fingers curling around it, willing him to feel how sincere her apology was. "I didn't know, Micah. I'm so, so sorry."

He gave a rough laugh. "The funniest thing was to get back here and find out that I'd somehow landed in the same hospital as my ex. Now that was kind of a kick in the teeth from the universe."

"Maybe this is *our* chance to make things right."

"Make things right?"

"Yes. To start off fresh. Not as a couple. But maybe as friends."

He stared at her. "You think it's possible for you and me to ever be friends?"

His words struck a nerve in her. She'd been trying to reach out to him, and to have him bat her words away like they meant nothing... A spike of anger went through her, and she found her fingers tightening on his arm in response. "Are you saying it's not possible?"

His palm cupped her nape, the heat from his skin going through her like an inferno. "Are you saying it is?"

She swallowed, her teeth grabbing at her bottom lip to stop it from trembling. "I—I want to try."

His fingers tunneled into her hair, and a shiver went through her. Maybe he was right. Maybe it wasn't possible, because what she felt right now wasn't remotely close to anything she would define as friendship.

"Yeah?" The gray of his eyes was flecked with much darker colors that shifted with his every mood. How could she ever have not recognized this man when he reappeared in her life? He was like no one else she'd ever met. He wasn't defined by the size of his nose or the conformation of his cheeks, the slope of his forehead or anything that supposedly distinguished one face from another. The difference was there, in his very being.

Suddenly, friendship or no, she wanted him to kiss her. Wanted to feel again the press of his mouth to hers. Maybe that's what all this talk about making things right was really about. Maybe it had nothing to do with righting past wrongs and was solely about what Micah made her feel. Made her want.

So she tipped her chin up with an air of defiance. "Yeah. I do."

One corner of his mouth tilted, and there went that glorious crease. She realized she'd been waiting to see it aimed at her for the last couple of hours. And here it was.

"Well, in that case." He slowly reeled her in, his gaze fastened on her lips.

Dio nei cieli. It was going to happen.

Her body flared to life as that first touch came. And come it did. This was no hesitant, questioning press. No waiting to see how she was going to react. This was war—a mind-blowing battle of one mouth against another. And she was up to the challenge, turning her head so that she could kiss him back, her hands going to his shoulders and dragging herself against him. If she could have climbed in his lap in that moment, she would have, but there was the gearshift and the whole two-separate-seats thing going on.

She opened her mouth as if anticipating exactly what he wanted and wasn't disappointed when his tongue swept in and took her by storm. A shivery need began thrumming through her, her nipples coming to hard peaks that cried out for his touch.

Her palms slid up and curled around his nape, the strands of his hair tickling across the backs of her hands as his head moved in time with what was happening inside her mouth.

A whimper erupted from her throat. She needed more. So much more.

Somehow she dragged her mouth from his and whispered his name.

"Yeah. I know."

She toyed with his hair, fingertips dragging across his skin, and he drew in several deep breaths. "If we don't stop now…"

This was the moment of truth. Did she venture down this path? Or did she retreat and head back to her own corner?

But, *Dio*, she wanted him. So, so badly. And suddenly she knew what she was going to say.

"Come back to my place."

He didn't pull away from her, but he did lean back a little to look into her face. "Are you sure?"

"No. But I know it's what I want right now."

"Hell, Lia." His eyes closed as if thinking it through. And when they opened again, there was a dark intensity in them that gave her her answer. Without a word, he untangled her arms from his neck, put the car in Reverse and pulled out of the parking spot.

He sent her a hard grin that said he was feeling the same thing she was. "In that case, you need to tell me where you live."

CHAPTER NINE

MICAH MADE THE trip to her apartment by darting through the streets and finding the paths with the fewest traffic lights. He hadn't forgotten how to navigate through this city.

Would he remember how to navigate her body with just as much ease?

Somehow she knew he would. Her hands wound together in her lap, gripping each other for support as she waited for him to make his way to the other side of town.

Why hadn't she suggested his hotel? It was closer.

Maybe because she needed to be on her own turf. To be able to keep herself rooted to reality and not go flitting off into some kind of fantasyland.

Wasn't that where she was already? A fantasyland that she'd never dreamed she could visit again.

His hand came off the gearshift and covered hers. "You okay?"

No, she wasn't, but there was no way he could know it was because she was frantic to arrive at their destination. So she wove her fingers of her left hand through his. "Yes. I just never realized how long this drive was before."

His teeth flashed. "I agree."

Then they were less than a mile away. "Turn left at this corner. The complex is about three blocks down on the right. You can park in my space. Three oh one."

Micah swung into the apartment building and followed her directions to the parking garage. It took her eyes a moment to adjust from the sun outside to the lights inside the structure, but her space was just around the corner. He carried her hand to the gear lever and sat it there for a minute, making her shiver as together they shifted the car into first. His thumb trailed across the side of her hand as he looked at her again. "Are you sure, Lia? Very, very sure?"

"Yes." She hoped he was asking about the sex and not just about parking in her space before realizing what a ridiculous thought that was. Of course it was about the sex.

He leaned over and kissed her again, and

this time his mouth was softer, exploring her on a level that made her insides knot and her heart pound. She didn't want to leave this car, but she was pretty sure her building had cameras inside the parking area, so she reached over and clicked the door release, the sound cracking through the intimate space.

When he looked at her, she attempted a smile. "Cameras."

"Ah. I thought for a second you might be running away."

Was that a reference to the way she'd left at graduation? But when she glanced at his face, she found it relaxed and sexy. There were no lines of tension that she could see.

"No. I just don't want the security people to get an eyeful." She gave a nervous laugh.

He got out of his door and made it to her side before she'd had a chance to swing her legs out. He reached for her hand and tugged her up and out of the car, one side of her jacket sliding down her arm. He reached for it, pulling it back into place. "Still cold?"

"No, not anymore."

She realized it was true. And although the parking garage was protected, she was pretty sure the warmth was left over from their earlier kisses more than from her coat.

He kept her hand, using his fob to lock the doors of his car. "There's an elevator?"

The way he said it made her swallow. "Cameras," she murmured.

That made him laugh, a sound that rumbled through her belly and drew a smile to her own lips.

"Oh, sorry! You weren't thinking in those terms."

He leaned down close to her ear. "You know I was. Remind me to get a place with no cameras. I'll take my chances."

He didn't elaborate, but she could pretty well imagine what he was willing to take his chances with. And right now, she agreed with him. Sex in an elevator with him would be better than any mile-high club ever invented.

They made it up the elevator without any incidents other than one very hot kiss, his body crowding hers against the wall and leaving her breathless. Then they were on her floor. She led him around the corner of the octagonal building and found her door. She unlocked both the locks and pushed it open. Then she heard a sound. *Oh, no.*

She put her hand against Micah's hip and attempted to push at him. "Wait behind me for a second."

He didn't budge. "Excuse me?"

"I don't want you getting hurt."

She thought she spied a blur of movement out of the corner of her eye. She quickly stepped in front of Micah, reaching for the hallway light.

"What the hell...?" His voice didn't sound any too pleased. But, dammit, she wasn't about to let anything spoil his mood. Or hers.

The light came on, and Lia spied her cat standing just to the side of them. Her tail was fluffed up in alarm. She took a step forward. "It's just me, girl."

"A cat? You're saving me from a cat?"

Samantha spotted him just about the time he asked his question. She stalked toward him, legs stiff, head pushed forward in a way that said she was nervous. It wasn't that Sam was mean. But she was scared of men and had been known to scratch first and ask questions later. The story from the shelter was that she'd been abused by some teenaged boys when she was a kitten. It had made her wary and untrusting.

Lia hadn't been abused, but her prosopagnosia had made her wary as well, so when she'd met the cat—soon after her breakup with Micah—they'd hit it off. Anytime she tried to leave the shelter's cat enclosure, Sam had clung to her leg, looking up at her with huge green eyes, her mouth opening and closing in a silent meow that was more like a plea. She hadn't been able to leave the young feline behind.

"She's not too sure about men."

He laughed, his warm breath washing over Lia's neck and sending Sam scurrying back a couple of paces. "And you suggested we come back to your place? Were we supposed to wind up in your bedroom or were you more interested in sending me to my doom?"

Rather than changing his mind or suggesting they go elsewhere, though, he stepped out from behind Lia and squatted down on his haunches. He held his hand out and murmured to the cat.

"No, don't—"

"Shh." He kept his arm where it was, and Sam inched forward, her long white fur standing up. "Come here, girl. I promise I'm good."

Yes, he was. And right now, all she wanted to do was grab him, sneak past her temperamental cat and close themselves in a bedroom to remind herself of just how good the man was. Although she remembered just about every minute of the time they'd spent together in the past.

Sam came forward another step as Micah continued to croon to her. His voice was as sweet as any country tune.

The cat came within clawing distance, and Lia tensed. But she didn't scratch. Instead, her neck stretched as far as nature would allow, and she sniffed Micah's fingers, then took another step forward. And another. And then the most remarkable thing happened. Samantha—man hater that she was—put her cheek against Micah's palm and purred.

"*Dio mio*, she never does this. Not with men."

He glanced up. "Had lots of men over here?"

"No, no of course not. That's not what I meant. It's more that the shelter told me she was hurt by guys in the past."

Micah slid his palm over Sam's head and stroked along her back. "Maybe she's checking out her competition."

"Competition?"

"For your affections." He turned to look at the cat. "Looks like she doesn't feel too threatened in that regard."

And she shouldn't be. Micah wasn't here

to win back her affections. He was here because things had gotten hot and steamy in his car. And she'd gotten enough of her senses back to be able to back out of anything happening. But she found she didn't want to. She wanted this night with Micah. She wasn't sure why. Maybe for the closure they hadn't gotten or maybe just to spend the night with someone who knew how to please her physically. She wasn't sure. But in the end, it didn't matter. She wasn't changing her mind.

"Micah…"

He glanced up, hand stopping midstroke. "Hmm?"

She licked her lips, ending it with her teeth pushing down on the corner of the lower one. "I'd like a little of what she's getting."

"Would you now?" He climbed to his feet, now ignoring the cat, who was winding herself around his legs and asking for more. "And is that all you want? A little petting?"

She wrapped her arms around his waist and pressed up against him. "No. And she might not be jealous, but maybe I am."

His hands pressed against her upper back, flattening her breasts against his chest before sliding down to just below her hips. His legs were slightly splayed, and when he applied just a bit of pressure, she felt everything. A hardness against her belly. A heat that couldn't be hidden even through layers of clothing.

He leaned down. "I kind of like you being jealous. Even if the other female involved is a cat." The words were said against her cheek, the syllables warming her skin and causing all kinds of yummy sensations to begin flashing in the lower part of her abdomen.

If her being jealous caused that kind of reaction from him, then she kind of liked it, too. "I'm just glad Sam didn't leave you with a present of another kind."

"Me, too. But sometimes old hurts fade and leave you able to trust again."

Something about the way he said that made a little niggle of worry appear in her stomach. Nothing major, just the flutter of butterfly wings. But then again, maybe those butterflies were signaling something entirely different. Maybe it was due to how he was making her feel with his nose sliding along the line of her jaw, the nibble of his teeth as he came up and touched those pearly whites to her lower lip. It was heavenly and soon pushed everything else to the side as she kissed him.

"Let's not talk about Sam anymore."

His hands slid into the hair on either side of her face, thumbs brushing the bones of her cheeks. "Kind of hard when she's down there reminding me of her presence."

His hips nudged her again, sending her thoughts somewhere else entirely.

"I'd like to be down there reminding you of my presence."

His thumbs stopped all movement. Then in a rush, he swept her up in his arms, managing to somehow maneuver past Sam, who thankfully hadn't taken issue with his sudden movement. "Bedroom?"

"There's only one. Straight ahead."

He strode past her living room and into the tiny hallway, moving into the bedroom and using his foot to close the door and exclude Samantha.

"She's not going to like that," Lia said with a laugh.

"Maybe not, but I kind of want you all to myself." He grinned. "And believe me, I need no reminders of your presence."

She reached up to touch that crease in his cheek as he moved over toward the bed.

His brows were up. "Should I play nice? Or naughty?"

"I think I'll need more information." Although she didn't, really. Naughty had always involved some kind of sexy play. And nice...well, that had been all about touch. And caring. And showing her exactly how much he loved her.

Loved her...

No. She didn't want that. Wasn't sure she could bear the way they'd made love during those times. So before he could answer, she blurted out, "I'll choose naughty."

Naughty she could handle. Naughty involved catching her up in a web of sensuality that was normally fast and hot and flamed her until she was sure she'd turn to a pile of ash.

He leaned down and caught her mouth in a hard kiss. "You may be sorry you asked for that."

"Never." She'd never been sorry for anything that they'd done together. She just wasn't sure she could rewind the clock to some of those days.

He kept kissing her until suddenly the bottom fell out. Or rather, she fell, hitting the bed with a soft *oomph* that left her dazed for a second or two before she gathered her senses and scrambled to her knees. "Hey!"

"Change your mind on naughty?"

"No." She could take whatever he dished out.

He leaned down and planted his hands on either side of her hips, his lips within inches of her own. "Good. I need a scarf. Where do you keep them now?"

She swallowed, memories coming back in a flood that almost overwhelmed her. *Dio*, they'd had so much fun back then.

This is not the past, Lia. Just enjoy the present for what it is.

She swung her feet over the edge of the bed and scooted forward, forcing him to stand up straight. "No scarves. Not just yet." With that she hooked her legs around the backs of his knees and crossed her ankles to keep him from moving away. "I think you need a little reminder of my presence."

"Lia…" His voice held an edge of warning that made her laugh.

Her bed was a four-poster monstrosity that she'd regretted getting because of how high the mattresses sat on it. Until right at this moment.

"If it's okay for you to restrain me, then

I think turnabout should be fair play, don't you agree?"

She reached for his belt and unbuckled it, sliding it out of the loops with a hiss. "Should your hands be behind your back for this?" She murmured the words aloud, as if talking to herself, while coiling the belt and laying it beside her on the bed. She tightened her legs as if getting his attention. "What do you think, Micah. How still can you be?"

His Adam's apple dipped as he swallowed. "Pretty damned still."

"Good to know." She plucked at the button of his trousers, sliding her hand along the front of his closed zipper. The air hissed between his teeth as she found the bulge hidden behind it. "Just trying to see if you can keep your word."

Her fingers trailed back up the way she'd come, and his eyes closed, his jaw tight. His hands fisted at his sides as if trying to hold himself together.

This time she didn't pluck. She undid the button and slid the zipper down in a smooth motion that made something at her center clench. She wasn't so sure about the sex play all of a sudden. Wasn't sure she didn't just want him to lay her down and take her.

But, *Dio*, she didn't want this to end. If he could stand the snail's pace, then so could she.

Hooking her fingers into his waistband, she slowly slid it down his hips until his slacks were perched on the muscles of his thighs. He had on black briefs, the hard ridge noticeable against the front of them. And there was a convenient opening right here. She slid her hand into the space and found warm, silky-smooth skin that was so welcome, so familiar that it made her teeth clench for a second. How many times had he used this to bring them both pleasure? How many times had she brought pleasure to him by what she was about to do?

No thinking about the past.

She freed him, glancing up to find his face was a hard, tight mask that made her frown, until she realized he really was trying to not come apart.

Same here, Micah. She wouldn't make him suffer too long, but she just couldn't resist.

"No hands, okay?"

He didn't answer but gave her a quick nod of assent, arms held rigidly at his sides.

They'd done this so many times before,

but right now, everything was new with the wonder of rediscovery.

She blew warm air over him, watching as a shudder rolled through his body. Yes. She remembered this.

Giving him little warning, she engulfed him in a smooth motion, the groan coming from above her fueling her need to drive him crazy. He wasn't supposed to use his hands, but she was allowed to use hers, so she slid them around his hips until she reached his ass and hauled him closer.

"Hell, Lia..."

He pulled free, watching her as she sat up. Then before she could do or say anything else, he'd flipped her onto her back, her head on the pillows. Then he stripped the rest of his clothes and donned a condom before climbing onto the bed with her.

He undressed her, pressing his lips to her skin as he revealed each part of her. Suddenly "naughty" was forgotten as his mouth found hers and his kisses grew urgent with need. He parted her legs and held himself at her entrance for several breathtaking seconds, ignoring the squirming of her body.

"Oh, Micah..."

He drove inside her with an intensity that pushed the air from her lungs. He paused, eyes closed, before cupping her head, his lids parting as he stared into her eyes. And what she saw there...

Need. Want. And some sort of longing that made her want to weep. Because she felt all those things, too. But she couldn't. Not now. Not when it was too late to go back.

So before she could get trapped in all those feelings and emotions, she reversed their positions until she was straddling his hips, engulfing him with her body the same way she'd done with her mouth. She moved, letting herself relish how it felt to be stretched and filled again. To take from him and to give back again and again. This time it was Lia who shut her eyes, focusing on the physical joining and praying she could evade anything that involved her heart or her head.

Hands gripped her waist, supporting her rise and fall and guiding the speed to match his need and hers. Leaning forward, she kissed his shoulder, dragging her teeth along his warm skin as if she couldn't get enough of him, and in reality she couldn't. She'd never been able to get her fill of this man.

Her movements grew quicker as she reached a set of rapids that carried her along, trying to remember to breathe as the ride grew wilder.

Micah's eyes were no longer on hers; instead it was as if he was focused on moving toward a goal that he didn't quite want to reach.

His name echoed in her head as she stared at his features, trying to distinguish what it was in his face that made him Micah. But all she could see was the blond hair that fell across his forehead, the hands with those long, talented fingers. His body with its strong arms and shoulders and taut, muscular abdomen. His scent. His voice. The unique gray of his eyes.

Those were the things that made him who he was in her eyes. And she wouldn't trade that for whatever it was that people saw in someone's face that made up good looks. Because what Micah had went far beyond any of that surface adornment of a straight nose or high cheekbones.

She sat up, still moving, and linked her hands with his, carrying them to the bed beside his head as she continued to move. A wave of sensuality swept over her as she looked at their joined fingers.

Micah chose that moment to open his eyes and look at her. And that was all it took. Her hips bucked wildly as a wave of need rushed through her, propelling her to a point beyond what she could see.

"Lia...oh, hell...yes!" He tugged his hands from hers and gripped her hips, holding her hard against him as he strained up into her. It was a picture she couldn't get out of her mind, of Micah pouring himself into her. Because he had, in a way that went far beyond sex and flowed into the very parts she'd tried so hard not to involve.

Her head.

And, *Dio*, her heart.

CHAPTER TEN

MICAH CAME TO with a sense of disorienta-
tion. It was dark, and he wasn't sure where
he was.

The hotel? No, this bed was different.
Softer. And...

Okay, his body definitely felt spent and
heavy, as if he couldn't move. Or maybe it
was that he didn't want to move.

Something tickled his face, like someone
drawing a feather duster over his cheek.

And then he heard it. A low rumble that
immediately identified itself.

A cat.

Then everything came rushing back to
him. This was Lia's house. And what they'd
done last night...

Was beyond anything he'd ever experienced.

A cold nose pushed against his chin, and
he smiled. Hated men, did she?

Not so much. He reached his hand up to pet her, his hand skimming along her back and curling around her tail. He sensed more than saw a dark figure curled up at the head of the bed.

He sat up. "Lia?" A moment of panic came over him. Had he hurt her somehow? They'd made love several times last night.

Moving over to where she sat, he tipped her chin up. "Are you okay?"

She nodded. "Just surprised it happened, is all."

Just surprised it happened. Well, hell, that pretty much mirrored his own thoughts, since he hadn't even known where he was when he sat up. "Me, too. And I'm sorry, but I can't quite bring myself to regret it, though."

"Me, either." She smiled. "And I can't get over the change in Samantha. It's amazing."

"Would you rather she woke me up in a different way?"

"No."

His smile was slow when it came, a sense of lethargic well-being that washed over him in a warm stream. "Would you rather I woke *you* up in a different way?" He glanced at the clock and saw that it was just after five. The sun hadn't come up yet, but it soon would, and it would more than likely chase away the magic of last night.

"I don't think Sam is going to let us go back to sleep. Sorry, but I had to let her in. She was meowing and sticking her feet under the door, and I was afraid she was going to wake you up. So I let her in. And she woke you up anyway."

"It's okay. And who said anything about sleep?" If he pushed in this direction, maybe his mind would stay away from some dangerous thoughts that were rolling around in it like boulders.

"But Sam…"

He climbed out of bed. "I bet we could sneak away and have a nice hot shower. And some alone time. Until one of us has to get dressed and be somewhere."

"Well, I don't have to be anywhere until eight."

"Same here. So that leaves us plenty of time."

"I can't promise Sam won't cause a ruckus outside the door."

He laughed. "I can't promise that you won't cause a ruckus *inside* the door."

"Me?" She punched his arm. "I seem to remember you making a whole lot more noise than I did."

"Did I? I don't remember it that way."
He got out of bed and swung her up in his
arms like he had at the beginning of the
night. It seemed fitting they should end it
the same way they'd started it. "So let's see
who causes more commotion this time."

With that, he carried her into the bathroom and shut them inside.

Hell, he was exhausted. This was the second night after leaving Lia's apartment that
he'd been kept awake by memories of what
they'd done. He'd tossed and turned, trying
to turn off his damned brain.

It hadn't worked. And Lia hadn't gone out
of her way to bump into him at the hospital.
Then again, he'd pretty much stuck to his
own wing, too, which was one floor above
hers. Glancing at the numbers he'd gotten
from neighboring hospitals of suspected pertussis cases, he was not pleased. A fourth
hospital had reported a case just this morning. A one-year-old girl was in critical condition with the illness.

He couldn't put it off any longer. He
needed to call Lia and see when she could
hang flyers with him. He picked up the
phone. But first he'd call the print shop and
see where they were on the flyers.

What was the guy's name who'd waited on them? Curtis, right?

A voice answered, but it was a woman. "Hi. This is Dr. Corday from Saint Dolores. We ordered some posters and flyers two days ago. Do you know if they're in? We ordered them from someone named Curtis, if he's there."

"Your order is in, but Curtis isn't. There was actually a family emergency with his wife, and he's just left to take her to the hospital."

Hadn't he said his wife was pregnant?

"Do you know which hospital?"

The woman's voice came back through. "Why, I think it was yours. It's the closest one to where he lives. And he had a card that one of your doctors had given to him. He called the number on it just as he was going out the door, so I don't know if he ever reached her."

"I'll check. And I'll be by to pick up that order a little later today."

"Okay. Please tell Curtis to call us if he needs anything."

"I will." When he hung up, he called Lia's number, only to have it go straight to voice mail. Damn. Had Curtis even been able to reach her?

Getting up, he headed out of his office. He would head downstairs and see if she was there. He knew he'd have to talk to her sooner or later, so maybe it would be easier if it was when other people were around. Just as he reached the door to the stairwell, his phone buzzed. Looking down at it, he saw that it was Lia. "Hey, I just tried to call you."

"I saw. I'm actually down here with Curtis Matthews from the print shop."

"Good. He did reach you, then."

There was a pause. "You knew he was trying to get a hold of me?"

"I called the shop to see if the order was ready, and the woman there said he was on the way to the hospital with his wife. I also called Douglas Memorial on the other side of town, and they've had a case of pertussis."

"Oh, God."

"What?"

"Curtis's wife. She's here, and she has a bad cough. I was hoping the illness wasn't spreading."

He rattled off a few curse words in his head. "It seems to be the case. She's not vaccinated."

"No. She's not. She and Curtis thought it

was no longer a threat, remember? I was just going to ask you to come and look at her."

"I was already on my way down. I'll be there in a minute."

He hung up and took the stairs two at a time before bursting through the door at the bottom.

Lia had recognized Curtis by the ankh ring he wore and by his black nail polish, although she'd already known he was coming by his frantic phone call. For all of Curtis's gothness, his wife was the opposite. She had soft, curly blond hair and had paired white skinny jeans with a loose white top that skimmed her pregnant belly. Her nail polish, unlike her husband's, was pink. They said opposites attracted, and this was one couple that she could definitely see that in. Except they were both really nice and obviously crazy about each other. Curtis sat next to the exam table and was constantly in contact with his wife via touch. Lia remembered a time when she and Micah were the same way when they were outside their med school classes.

Two nights ago, they'd been the same. She'd woken up in a dark room and realized that Micah's arm was around her. She'd flat-out panicked, then realized she could hear Sam meowing outside the bedroom door. It was the perfect excuse to let her in and then crawl back in bed and watch him sleep.

The softness she saw as he lay there—one hand draped over his belly, his muscles loose and relaxed—was a sharp contrast to the commanding man she knew at the hospital and from med school.

She headed back into the exam room when she heard some hard coughing. Curtis looked worried. "Can she bring on contractions? She's feeling something going on in her stomach."

"It's unlikely, but I've got a call in for the obstetrician. It's just going to be a few minutes because she's in the middle of a delivery. I know you said this is your first baby, correct?"

"It is." Jenny was sitting up, blowing in and out. "I should have gotten the vaccine, but I was going to do everything natural. He wanted to come to Saint Dolly's for the delivery, but I wanted to have a home water birth with just Curtis there. We were still in discussions about it." A smile played on her face as she glanced at her husband.

A little alarm bell went off. "Have you been in touch with a midwife or a doula?"

Curtis spoke up. "We always meant to, but we're both so busy with our jobs and work different schedules, so we just haven't yet. And our families don't approve of home births, which is why I wanted to come to the hospital."

That was hard. Lia's parents had always been so supportive of her, outside of her dad really pressing her to get a system together for recognizing people. But once she hit adulthood, her dad had started wearing a bright green crocheted bracelet, a counterpart for his wife's pink one. A wave of overwhelming emotion had swamped her when he'd showed up at her graduation ceremony with it on. She'd cried. Then her mom had cried with her. Her dad had remained stoic, but she was pretty sure she saw moisture in his eyes as he'd hugged her and whispered, "Congratulations, *figlia*. I'm so proud of you."

A knock at the door sounded, and then Micah came into the room. He donned a mask and gloved up. "Hi, Curtis. It's nice to see you again, although not so much under these circumstances."

"I know. Your order is in, by the way."

His eyes crinkled above the mask. "I know. I called the shop and found that you had come to visit us here at the hospital, rather than the other way around."

"Not by choice."

Micah pulled a chair up. "So tell me what's going on?"

He didn't ask Lia, but she wouldn't have expected him to. It was good for him to hear it from Curtis and Jenny.

They gave him a quick rundown with Jenny ending the story by saying Curtis had come home talking about whooping cough going around. "I've had a bad cough for about a week and started to get worried that I could make the baby sick."

This time Micah did look at her. "Did you do a nasal swab?"

"I did it a few minutes ago and sent it down to the lab."

"Good." He turned back to Jenny. "Do you know if you were exposed to anyone with a cough?"

"I make custom cakes at a bakery for parties. There are always people milling around, so I don't know. I've never thought much of someone coughing."

He nodded. "Could you get a list together of people who came in to order cakes?"

She started to answer then stopped when a set of racking coughs went through her.

She held her hand to her belly until she was done. Lia handed her a bottle of water, which the patient drank from. "I can get a list, but we don't really write on the order forms if the person called or came in in person."

"I can understand that. Any kind of list will help, because we can check it against people who have come in complaining of a cough."

"I'll call them right now and ask them to text over a list. From how far back?"

Micah frowned as if thinking. "About three weeks. It's not contagious after that period of time. We won't do anything with it until we know for sure that you have it."

"Okay."

He gave her a smile. "Thanks. It'll take a few hours to get the results back. Are you two okay hanging around at the hospital in one of the isolation rooms until then? We can make sure you get something to eat and drink. If the results come back negative for both of you, then you'll be free to go. But we recommend you both get vaccinated, since we're seeing an increase in cases all over the city. The disease isn't as bad for adults, but for babies…let's just say it's bad news."

"Can I be vaccinated this late in the pregnancy?"

"Yes, although we normally recommend it be done sooner. But you'll pass the antibodies to your baby, and it will help protect him or her for the first two months of their life. At which time they can be vaccinated. We had a close call with a baby here at the hospital. She ended up living, but it was touch and go for a while."

Jenny looked at her husband with brows lifted. "I want to get it. For the baby's sake."

"I will, too. I don't think I've had one since I was a kid."

"Great. If you could help spread the word, it would be much appreciated." Micah's glance included both of them.

Curtis nodded. "After you came in, I told my boss what had happened, and he said we can put a flyer up at the print shop."

"And I'll ask the bakery if it's okay. They're kind of stinky about anything that would make people nervous or anxious, but this is important."

"Yes, it is. Thank you both."

Watching Micah interact with the young couple made a sense of admiration swell up in her. She bet he'd done great work in Ghana with his trachoma campaign.

Lia motioned to the door. "If you'll both come with me, I'll show you to a room that's a little more comfortable with this one. And I'll run to the cafeteria and get you both something to eat while you wait on the ob-gyn to get done with her delivery."

"Thank you."

She led them down the hallway to a small private waiting room that had eight chairs. They normally used the room for family groups that were waiting for news of relatives who were in serious or critical condition. "Don't be alarmed, but I'm going to put a sign on the door stating that this is an isolation room and that it's only to be entered by people who are gowned and masked. Just until we know for sure."

Lia picked up one of the nearby red-framed signs and wrote Curtis and Jenny's names on it along with the date and time. When she was done, she put tape on it and affixed it to the outside of the door. "Now, Micah and I are going to see if we can find something for you to eat. What sounds good?"

Jenny shrugged. "Maybe just some soup and crackers. My stomach is kind of in knots."

"I totally understand. Do you want some juice to go with it?"

"Some apple if they have it."

Micah had grabbed a piece of paper and was scribbling down their order. Or at least that's what she thought he was doing.

"Curtis?"

"I don't know that I can eat."

Lia patted him on the arm. "I know, but it's best to keep your strength up for your wife and baby's sakes."

"Okay, just a sandwich and chips, then. Maybe chicken of some kind. And a cola."

"Great. We won't be long."

She and Micah went out of the room, making sure the door was all the way shut. "Thanks for coming down," she said. "What do you recommend we do?"

"Exactly what you're already doing. Did they come in a side door like Sassy and her family?"

"Yes. Thank goodness Curtis thought to call and didn't just walk into the ER with her. I'm hoping it's not pertussis."

"So am I."

Although whooping cough didn't normally cause complications during pregnancy, there was always the danger of giving birth with an active infection. And the cough could strain abdominal muscles, which were already stretched by late pregnancy, making for a very uncomfortable situation.

They went down to the first floor, where the hospital cafeteria was located, and got some chicken noodle soup and juice for Jenny and a turkey and cheese sandwich for her husband.

"I'm done for the day, so I'm going to sit up there with them and wait on their results. I can only imagine how scary this is for both of them."

"I'll run over and grab the print order and get the posters at least up in the hospital. Then I'll be back to see if we can run down that list of customers from the bakery. Since Curtis isn't coughing, I'm not as worried about the print shop."

Lia took hold of the bags with the food in it. "Sounds good."

Before she could walk away, Micah stopped her with a hand to the arm. "I haven't seen you the last couple of days. I wanted to make sure Samantha wasn't traumatized by her unexpected run-in with a man."

The question made her laugh.

For some reason, she'd expected him to ask her how she was doing, or worse, apologize for what they'd done at her apartment. It was part of the reason why she'd been avoiding him for the last two days. But only part of it. In reality, she'd had no idea what she was going to say if he did either of those things.

"Sam is just fine. No worse for wear."

"And you? No worse for wear?"

Ah, and there was the question du jour. Asking how she was.

"No worse for wear." She forced a smile. "I'm a pretty resilient girl."

"I'm glad. I just wanted to make sure we knew where the other stood."

She blinked. Did he? That wasn't exactly the question he'd asked her. And thank God he hadn't. Because right now she had no idea what her response would have been. Right now, she didn't want to examine where they stood. On a professional level or a personal one. Because if her suspicions were right, she was having an awful time keeping the past and present in their respective corners.

She'd missed him. The last several weeks had proven that beyond a shadow of a doubt. Watching him interact with patients and hold baby Sassy, watching him interact with her cat…and experiencing his touch all over again…well, it made her want to go back and change the way things had ended between them.

But she couldn't. And right now, she wasn't sure if she was going to be able to keep him from realizing that. Or what she would do if Micah somehow guessed the truth.

CHAPTER ELEVEN

JENNY'S TEST TWO days ago had come back negative, and they'd sent the relieved couple home after vaccinating both of them. The hospital had had some names of midwives that worked with the medical center, and they had promised to contact someone on the list.

That was the good news. The bad was that two more area hospitals had called in cases of whooping cough. Nashville was now up to twenty, with most of the cases congregated around Saint Dolly's hospital. Micah and Lia were scheduled to go out once she finished her last procedure of the day and hang flyers in local businesses and in areas where the public gathered. The CDC had also mounted a television campaign aimed at public awareness, and Micah was helping track cases of exposure.

Lia's artwork was also getting some media

exposure, after a reporter had spied one of the framed prints hanging on the wall at the hospital. And of course Arnie hadn't been able to resist saying that a member of the hospital staff had done the design on it. Lia had been mortified. But at least they hadn't given the media her full name. But since Curtis had talked her into signing the original, it was probably only a matter of time until someone realized who the artist was.

His phone buzzed, and he glanced down to see a text from her.

I'm done. Ready whenever you are.

He smiled. She always had been short and to the point. Most of the time he'd found it amusing. Except when she'd broken things off with him. That had been a killer. It had taken going to Ghana to get over her. He knew for a fact he couldn't have done it here in Nashville. Seeing her day after day would have been impossible. Running into her after that long of an absence had been enough of a shock.

And sleeping with her?

Well, that had been a much nicer shock than the original. It seemed like they'd kind of gotten their footing again around each other. Maybe sleeping together hadn't been the huge mistake he'd originally thought it was. Maybe it really had given him some closure after all these years and would allow them to do what she'd suggested when she said they could start off fresh...as friends. At the time he'd been incredulous that she could even suggest that. Then of course that had led to them spending the night together, and definitively *not* as friends.

He wasn't yet sure what it all meant. Or how he felt about it. Or her. But maybe they could walk it back and actually become congenial. It seemed like they were on their way to doing just that. And he was looking forward to going out with her this afternoon to hang the flyers, which was worlds away from how he'd felt when he'd seen her at that Valentine's Day benefit.

He typed on his keypad to respond to her text.

I'll meet you in the lobby with the goods.

He followed the words with a laughing emoji, smiling when she responded in kind.

See? Friends.

While most of his brain accepted that as a very real possibility, there was a small portion that was standing back with its arms folded waiting for everything to implode in his face like it had three years ago. Except they weren't a couple now. She couldn't break up with him again. Actually, there wasn't much she could do other than avoid him. Or quit.

That made him frown. Surely it would never get to that point? So far they'd been able to remain on decent terms. So he'd just have to make sure he kept it that way.

He got down to the lobby with an attaché filled with weatherproof flyers. Hopefully between this and what the CDC and other hospitals were doing, they'd be able to prevent the outbreak from spreading even further. Fortunately, there were still no deaths attributed to the illness.

She grinned as she walked up to him. "Is this where I say, 'Hi, honey, I'm home'?"

Honey.

He couldn't stop himself from recoiling at the word—the empty endearment his mother had used on him from time to time. Empty because there was no true affection behind it. She used it on everyone who came across her path. And to hear Lia use it in the same flippant, meaningless way...

It's just a word. It means nothing.

He gritted his teeth and worked past the raw emotions that were swirling through him.

"Micah? What's wrong?"

He needed to just shut up and not say anything. But to do that seemed wrong. Especially since she was apt to use that word again. She used to when they were together, and he'd never complained. But maybe he should have. Should have been more open about how life with his parents had been. Instead, he'd hidden it, thinking that Lia could help him get through it. Looking back, it hadn't been fair to pile that kind of expectation onto her shoulders. Especially since she hadn't even known she was carrying that particular load. The truth was, he'd hidden the truth because he'd been embarrassed, especially after seeing how loving Lia and her parents were with each other. It made his own household seem like a farce. Like some sitcom of dysfunction that never really resolved.

And since his and Lia's connection had weighed so heavily toward the physical, he never bothered to ask himself if he could even have a healthy emotional relationship with her—or anyone. But after that breakup? Hell, he'd asked himself that question repeatedly. Because apparently something had been off that he hadn't been able to see at the time.

And now that they were supposedly "friends"? Maybe it was time to come clean. At least a little bit.

"Nothing. I'm just not overly fond of that word."

"Word? What word?"

Now he was feeling a bit ridiculous for saying anything. "*Honey.* My mom just used it whenever she was trying to talk me into doing something. Or hoping I'd go away."

She blinked. "Oh, Micah. I'm sorry, I didn't know. I'm pretty sure I used to call you that…before. Why didn't you say anything?"

"I don't know. I probably should have."

"All right. I'll try to remember." She paused a few seconds. "She really made you feel like she wanted you to go away?"

He shrugged, stepping closer to her to let someone get past them. "I'm sure all kids feel like that from time to time."

Her brows went up, as if she wasn't sure what to say to that. But she didn't try to pull any more confessions from him, for which he was thankful.

Instead, she finally just said, "I won't use that word again. Thank you for telling me."

There were a few awkward moments while they tried to figure out their footing again. But finally she smiled and pulled her keys out of her purse and held them up. "So...my place or yours?" A little bell tinkled as she shook the keys, making him forget for the moment how his body had jolted to life at her question.

Hadn't he heard that bell at Lia's house the night he'd stayed over?

"I thought you put that back on Samantha's collar."

"I did. But I found it in the bedsheets this morning. I don't know how she keeps getting it off."

Man, the image of Lia sprawled across rumpled sheets was moving through his skull at a snail's pace, refusing to be hurried off his mental screen. The jolt he'd felt a minute ago returned full force. He knew exactly what she looked like when she slept. And so did his body.

To throw his mind off track, he reached over to finger the little bell, forcing himself to look for a spot where there was a fissure or break, but there was nothing. "Has it ever fallen off your key chain the way it does her collar?"

"Nope. I don't know what its deal is."

Avery's earlier words about Samantha's witchy ways came back to him.

"Maybe the problem is with the ring on her collar."

Her teeth worked at her lip for a minute like she did whenever she was thinking. Micah had to glance away when his thoughts veered back to things that had nothing to do with cats or bells.

"I'll have to check it when I get home." She seemed to shake off a thought. "So back to the question. Are we taking my car or yours?"

It was a different question than she'd voiced a moment ago and didn't flood his brain with a rush of endorphins this time. But he'd already known she wasn't talking about homes. Just cars.

"If I remember right, your little blueberry was kind of a tight fit."

Oh, hell. That hadn't come out quite right.

The impish smile she gave him made the sides of her nose crinkle. "Yes. It was kind of a snug ride, wasn't it?"

The words hit their mark, snagging his thoughts and taking them hostage.

She did not mean it that way. But that smile was the same one she'd given him in the past. The exact. Same. Smile.

No matter how many times he tried to banish the memory of just how snug that particular ride had been, a heady, terrifying warmth began to pool in his groin. It had nowhere to go…but up.

Dammit! He needed to pull himself together.

"We'll take my car." He bit the words out with a fierceness that didn't go unnoticed.

Lia's smile faltered. "Are you sure you want me to come with you?"

"Yes, sorry. I didn't mean that to sound the way it did."

"It's okay. My words a few minutes ago didn't come out exactly right, either."

Ah…so had she not realized how her words had come across until now? But she'd had that knowing little grin. When he glanced at her, he could swear he saw a tinge of pink in her cheeks. Maybe she had meant them—as a joke—but his reaction had been so over-the-top that she'd probably had second thoughts about trying to make him laugh.

He sighed. Maybe his hopes of being friends was destined to fail.

Pushing the door, he held it open to let her go ahead of him.

The frigid blast of air hit him in the chest, the cold putting the deep freeze on some very overheated parts. He drew in a deep breath or two, letting the door swing shut behind him.

The weather had taken an unexpected turn, dropping back below freezing, which wasn't too unusual for Nashville, seeing as it was still only the end of February. A severe weather alert had pinged on his phone a while ago, warning folks to look out for slick spots on the roadways due to the rain that had fallen during the morning commute.

Pulling his coat around him as they moved through the parking lot, he unlocked the doors to the car before they got there.

Once they were inside, he realized they should have taken the blueberry. Because they'd had that spectacular kiss in this car. Right before he'd gone up to her apartment.

It was too late now. He was stuck here with her for the next couple of hours. He pulled out onto the road and headed south.

"I spent part of today calling local businesses, and I have the names of some places that are willing to put up our flyers. I mapped them in the order of our route."

"Great. If you want to hand me the map, I can help navigate."

"It's in the front pocket of the attaché."

"Which is where?"

"It's in the back seat. Let me pull over and get it."

Great. Smart work, Micah.

"No problem. I'll just unbuckle for a minute. Try not to send me flying through the windshield with any fast stops, though." She unhooked her belt and then twisted in her seat, hanging over, trying to reach the bag, which was behind his seat. Something soft pressed against his shoulder, and his jaw tightened, trying not to think about what it was. He rounded a curve and sent her bottom swinging into him instead.

"Damn. Sorry."

No choice. He hooked one arm over her derriere to anchor her in place while she reached for the bag.

"Got it."

He lifted his arm to let her slide back into her seat. "Thanks for hanging on to me."

"No problem." But it was. Because his thoughts were right back where they'd started. With her. And him. Doing very naughty things in a very snug place.

She pulled the sheet of paper from the front of the bag and glanced at it. "Oh, wait. The first one is on the next block. Papa's Pizza Parlor."

"Okay. Hold on."

He swung into the correct lane and found the place almost immediately. Parking, they took a flyer in, talking to the owner for a minute before heading back to the vehicle. Maybe they hadn't needed two people to undertake such a simple task, but it was easier and safer to have someone looking for the places he'd called.

They returned to the car, and she glanced at the sheet. "We're headed to the park on Thirty-First next. It's about a mile away."

A drop of sleet hit his windshield. Great. "Hopefully we won't get much of this."

He pulled over to the curb and started to put the vehicle in Park only to have her say, "Let me just jump out and staple it to the information board. You did get permission to hang it, didn't you?"

"I did. But I can do it. I have a staple gun in the main pocket of my bag."

"Just stay here, then you won't have to turn the car off. I'll just be a minute." She hopped out of the car with the flyer and the staple gun and headed to the large plywood structure where people hung notices for different events.

She pushed the stapler, and evidently nothing happened, because she turned it toward her and looked at it before setting the flyer down, stepping on it to keep it from blowing away and giving the gun a shake before opening the cartridge and looking inside. He was just about to get out of his car to help when she picked the flyer back up and tried again. This time she was successful. She'd just turned around to come back to the car when it started sleeting in earnest. Putting her coat over her head, she sprinted toward the car and almost made it when she slipped and went down backward.

"Hell!" In a split second, he was out of the car and jogging toward her. She was already on her feet by the time he reached her. "Are you okay?" He had to shout to be heard as the sleet gave way to torrential rain.

"I'm fine." But when she went to take a step, she grimaced before shifting her weight back onto her other foot. "I think I just twisted my ankle. I'll be okay."

"Put your arm around my waist." The rain was still coming down, and by the time she hobbled to the car, their clothes were plastered to them.

The gutter between the car and the sidewalk had become a river, and there was no way she was going to be able to step across it with her ankle like it was, so, still holding on to her, he reached over and opened the door, then before she could protest, he lifted her, stepping into the rushing water and setting her on the seat. He closed the door, then slogged his way to the other side of the car and got in, turning the heat on high. Then he looked over at her, and they both burst out laughing.

The rain was pounding the top of the car and sluicing down the windshield. He turned his wipers on high. "Well, that didn't quite go as planned, and I don't think anyone is going to let us in looking like this."

She glanced over at him. "*Dio*, your pants are so... I'm sorry you had to get in that water."

"I'll be fine. But I should probably get you home before you freeze and that ankle swells."

Despite the heat pouring from the vents, Lia's jaw was quivering as her teeth chattered. From the cold? Or had she really done something to her ankle?

"Maybe we should get that foot X-rayed."

"No, it'll be fine. I'm just freezing."

And that settled it. He pulled slowly from his spot, trying to watch the traffic as his tires sprayed water in all directions.

"Aim those vents toward you."

She reached forward and did it before widening her eyes. "Oh, no!"

"What?"

Lia held up his stapler. "It may be ruined after hitting the ground and getting rained on."

His stapler. His *stapler*. She was something else. "That's the last thing I'm worried about. We're about three minutes away from your complex."

"Just park in my spot again."

A feeling of déjà vu settled over him, along with a sense of doom. To be in that apartment again… But what was he going to do? Drop her off at the front door to the building and drive away? The least I could do was make sure she was okay. Get her settled in with a hot cup of coffee and check her ankle.

They made it to the parking garage, which, thank heavens, was covered and led directly into the building through a covered corridor. He parked and came around to her side of the door. As she stepped out, she grimaced as she tried to put weight on her ankle again.

"This is so stupid. I can't believe I was that clumsy."

"You weren't clumsy. I almost slipped, too." He smiled. "So, do you want to be carried in—which is my preferred method—or are we going back to the arm around the waist?"

"Definitely arm around the waist. Cameras, remember?"

"I seem to remember it didn't stop us from putting on quite a preshow as we went up the elevator last time."

"Ugh. Don't remind me. Every time I go by the security guard, I picture him watching that scene. Or worse, taping it and playing it for his friends."

"He's probably seen it all before. Keys?"

She handed him her keys and her purse before hesitating and then finally putting her arm around his waist. Was it that hard to touch him? Or was she really just embarrassed about the cameras?

He supported her with his other arm as they slowly made their way to the elevator. She gasped when they had to step up onto a different level once they got inside. Dammit. It would have been less painful to have let him carry her. Not to mention faster. They must look quite the sight. His shoes were literally squelching with each step, and though he didn't look behind him, he was pretty sure he was leaving wet tracks across the pristine surface of the lobby floor. Lia's long ponytail, which had been neat and tidy when they'd left the hospital, was now canted toward the left, and she had a big patch of mud on her left cheek.

A guard came running from somewhere, his hand on his hip—where he kept what looked like a Taser. "Dr. Costa, are you okay?"

"I'm fine. It's okay." Lia frowned as if realizing what a sight they must be, then shut her eyes for a few seconds. Micah could picture exactly what she was thinking—the preshow was nothing compared to this. "I just sprained my ankle. Dr. Corday was kind enough to help me get home."

"Do you want me to get the wheelchair we keep in the lobby?"

She gave a short laugh. "At this point, I'm afraid of somehow destroying that, too."

"You won't," the guard assured her, his tone worried.

"I'm fine, but thank you for offering."

What had she destroyed? The stapler?

That was nothing. Maybe she was worried about his car.

"Hey, my leather seats are pretty tough, if that's what's bothering you. They'll dry as good as new."

"As good as new."

Was she sure she hadn't somehow hit her head? He needed to get her up to her apartment so he could check her over.

They got onto the elevator, and the trip to the third floor seemed to take forever, unlike the last trip, when it had sailed up at the speed of light. Finally the door opened, and he splayed out her keys, searching for the right one, the little bell from Samantha's collar jingling. That's right. Hopefully the cat liked him as well today as she had the last time. The last thing he needed was her adding to the confusion.

He inserted the key into the lock, and the mechanism released, allowing the door to swing in. Helping her inside, he toed off his wet shoes and reached over to turn on the light. He closed the door again, latching it. "Where do you want me to take you?"

"To the bedroom." As if realizing how that sounded, she said, "I want to get out of these clothes. Why don't you go into the bathroom and do the same?"

As if she could feel his grin, she looked up, and for the first time since her sad little comment to the guard, she smiled. "You know what I mean."

He laughed. "Then maybe you should *say* what you mean. But I get it. The only problem is I don't have a change of clothes here, and I doubt you want me parading around wearing…" He purposely allowed the words to trail away.

"There's a terry robe in there that you can use. If it doesn't fit front ways, you could always pretend it's a hospital gown where the opening goes to the back."

Perfect. "Do you need help changing?"

"I think I'm good. If I need help, I'll yell."

She wouldn't. Of that he was sure. He helped her to her room and left her standing in the middle of the bedroom while he went over to her dresser.

"What are you doing?"

"Getting you some clothes."

"You don't have to—"

"I do," he muttered. "Unless you want to stand here while we argue about it."

"Okay. But don't look."

"At…?"

"The stuff in my drawers."

Did she realize how ludicrous that sounded?

"Do you want me to promise to go by feel rather than by sight?" He let one side of his mouth quirk, and her face immediately turned colors.

What was that all about?

He opened one drawer and found socks. The next one had what he was looking for. Hmm…what color? The array before him was dazzling; his fingers ventured in to touch and—

"You're looking."

Yes, he was. But what did she expect a man to do? He grabbed the first pair his fingers had trailed across and started to close the drawer when he heard a screech. "No, not that pair!"

Hmm? He looked at what he was holding in his hand. Okay, there was barely anything there, except for…strings. What exactly what this used for?

He tried again, taking another pair out, a bit more gingerly this time. Okay, these looked like normal, albeit frilly underwear. He held them up for her approval.

"Yes, they're fine."

He found her a bra and jeans and a comfy-looking shirt with the words *Nashville Chick* splashed across it.

"Avery bought that for me." Said as if he

expected an explanation. He didn't. But it had given him a little too much pleasure to pick out things for her to wear. He remembered doing that on some of their "naughty" nights when the sky had been the limit. Those string-a-ling undies would have been perfect for one of those sessions.

Stop it, Micah.

"Are you sure you can tackle putting them on?"

"I am positive."

Something in her face made him dubious, but she pointed her finger toward the bathroom before letting her arm fall back to her side. He doubted she'd call for help even if she landed in a heap on the floor. Giving her a final glance, he made his way to the bathroom, only to find his way blocked by Samantha, who'd—sans warning bell—sneaked up on him. "Hey, girl. I wondered where you were. Remember me?"

As if answering, she moved in, her purr box starting up immediately as she sniffed the bottom of his sodden trousers and his bare feet. "You don't want me petting you right now. I'm pretty wet."

He tried to go into the bathroom, only to have her follow him inside. Hmm… From what Lia had said, he wasn't sure about reaching down and trying to set her out-side, so he let her stay. "Just so you know, scratching at anything you see in here is for-bidden, got it?"

As the cat wandered around the small area, he shed his clothes, finding the bath-robe hanging where she said it would be. It was terry cloth all right. But it was pink and had a huge hummingbird on one side of the chest. Well, there was no way he was pull-ing his soaked clothes back on. So he took the robe from its hook and slid his arms into the sleeves, the shiny ruffled edging com-ing to the middle of his forearm. Thankfully when he went to wrap it around his waist it was big enough to cover him, although there wasn't much fabric to spare, and the bottom edge hung above his knees.

Hell. This would have been a winner for comedy night if they'd had one when they'd been together.

When he cinched the pink belt and ex-ited the bathroom, Samantha followed him into the bedroom. Except he was shocked to find Lia standing exactly where he'd left her. In her wet things with the dry ones lying across the bed. Her face was paler than he'd ever seen it.

"Lia? What's wrong?"

* * *

She heard Micah's voice through a fog and looked at his face. She realized she'd been standing there, lost in thought about him. About their past. About what they'd done in this room not that long ago.

She was so tired. Tired of everything. Of the scramble for recognition that seemed to go on every time she turned around. Of how other people seemed to sail effortlessly through life, recognizing their friends and family immediately. Not having to pretend until you could finally work out who the person was.

She'd only known who Curtis was because of his ankh ring...the security guard because of his uniform.

Even Micah, who was someone she'd once loved.

Samantha rubbed against his legs as she stared at him. At the hair plastered against his head. At the strong shoulders hidden beneath her robe.

Someone she still loved.

Oh, God. How could she let herself do this all over again? She'd only end up disappointing him when he finally discovered the truth about why she hadn't wanted to go to Ghana, about why she'd really broken things off with him.

"I—I can't. I just can't."

"You can't what? Get dressed?"

She just shook her head, unable to say any of the things that were spinning out of control in her head.

He took hold of her shoulders and studied her face.

Her damned face! The face that she didn't even recognize when she looked in the mirror. She only knew it was her in the reflection because she was standing there in front of it. She could see the features. Knew what a nose, eyes and mouth were, but put them all together on a person, and they all looked the same, with no identifiable differences.

As if he'd seen something that she couldn't begin to vocalize, he folded her in his arms and held her close. Rubbed her back, skimmed a lock of hair off her face.

"I'm going to undress you, okay?"

She forced herself to nod, even though he probably had no idea what was really going through her head. Hell, she didn't know, either. Only knew that she still loved Micah.

And that she shouldn't.

Gentle fingers were on her skin as he pulled her blouse up and over her head,

undid her bra and slid it off her shoulders.
She felt another shirt come down over her,
covering her chest. He did the same with her
shoes, pants and underwear. The old came
off and new things replaced them. Things
that weren't embedded with cold. A cold that
had moved to envelop her soul.

"Do you want some coffee?"

Her head wagged back and forth as if it
had a mind of its own.

"You're shivering. Let me get your hair
down and get you into bed." He gently removed the elastic from her hair and slid his
fingers through it to loosen any tangles.

She sighed and closed her eyes. It felt
good. So good.

Arms scooped her up as if she were a precious piece of china and walked with her
across the room. This time he didn't drop
her onto the surface of the bed. He gently
pulled down the covers and placed her on
it. When he went to let her go, though, she
gripped the lapels of the robe. "Don't leave,
Micah. Please."

"I won't." He kissed her forehead. "Slide
over and I'll get in with you."

She scooted over, and Micah crawled
in beside her. Her ankle throbbed in time
with the beating of her heart, but having him

next to her was better than any pain reliever known to man. He'd always been a balm to whatever hurt. And right now, everything hurt. Everything…except him.

Wrapping her arms around him to keep him close, the shivering gradually faded away, and she allowed herself to relax fully into him. Closed her eyes and trusted he'd still be there when they reopened.

Then she let all her thoughts and fears float toward the ceiling as she focused on the one constant in her life at this moment in time.

Micah.

CHAPTER TWELVE

LIA OPENED HER eyes with a start. It was still dark, and the apartment was silent. Micah hadn't left. He was lying facing her, one leg thrown over hers, his hand clasping her arm as if afraid she was going to disappear into the night.

She loved him. The realization from earlier this evening sweeping back over her.

Dio. How could she let this happen again?

She hadn't *let* it happen again. It was the same love she'd had for him before. It was why she'd never dated after he'd left.

Her hand trailed down his arm. And Micah. Did he still feel something for her? He wasn't married. Had traveled an awful long distance to get away from her.

Had anything really changed, though? She was the same fearful person she'd been the last time they met. Even if he still cared about her—

He stirred in his sleep and pulled her closer.

Maybe she could put those thoughts on hold for a little while.

She leaned forward and kissed his jaw. The stubble tickled her lips in a way that was more delicious than words. But it was a deliciousness she remembered. A hunger that only he'd been able to satisfy. He murmured something, and then his eyes came open with a speed that made her blink. They zeroed in on her, pupils constricting.

"What are you doing?"

"Kissing you."

He leaned back, a frown pulling his brows together. "I can see that. Are you okay? You were kind of a mess last night."

"Yes, and I'm really sorry about that. I think I was cold and then just got overwhelmed. Nothing that day had gone right, and I—I suddenly realized how much my prosopag…" She stopped. *Dio*, she'd almost blurted out the truth. But maybe he should know. He deserved to know. She'd kept it from people all her life, except for a select few who knew her daily battle. Her parents. Her sister. Avery had guessed the truth and made her spill, but no one else ever had. And no one in her professional realm seemed to notice, thanks to the lanyards they all wore at work and the tells she'd worked out on those she saw on a daily basis. She'd become adept at living a lie.

Her dad would be proud of her.

But she wasn't her uncle, and she was no longer sure her father's solution had been the best one for her.

She would tell Micah and see what happened. Just not this moment. If he rejected her, then she would at least be able to look back on this memory and hold it close.

And if he didn't push her away? If he still cared about her once he knew?

She took a deep breath and picked up her sentence again, changing it slightly. "I suddenly realized how very alone I feel."

His hands cupped her face, throat working for a second. "Oh, Lia. I am sorry. God's honest truth, I know what that feeling is like." He leaned down to kiss her. "But you're not alone right now."

"No, you're right. I'm not."

One kiss turned to two, and a shuddery laugh erupted when Samantha decided to insert herself between them, purring and rubbing her head on his shoulder.

"Is it safe for me to pick her up and set her outside? I don't want to leave your place tonight missing an eye. I'm going to need all my senses for what I plan to do next."

Anticipation whispered up her spine, and she smiled. "Somehow I think my cat has fallen in love with you."

"Just your cat?" The lightness of his smile took any heaviness from his words.

But what if she wanted heavy?

Her breath hissed in. *Don't ruin this. Let him tell you first.* So she gave a laugh that she hoped was equally light and said, "That's for me to know."

He leaned down by her ear. "And for me to find out."

Climbing out of bed, he scooped the cat up. She curled next to his chest and just ate it all up.

Lia smiled and whispered, "I can't blame you, Sam."

He set her gently outside the door and shut it.

Then he came back to bed and started to slide back under the covers before thumbing the terry cloth collar of the robe he still wore. "I have to tell you, this is the most uncomfortable contraption I have ever worn to bed."

"You never used to wear anything."

One brow went up. "I still don't. But

last night, there were extenuating circumstances."

"Those are all gone. So go ahead."

"Are you sure?"

When she nodded, he undid the bow in front, and as the fabric slithered down his body, she couldn't help but run her gaze over him. He was perfect. Gorgeous. And for right now, he was all hers.

And later?

She could worry about that in the morning.

This time when he slid under the covers, she reached for him, finding his mouth with hers. And unlike the last time, there was nothing playful about his kiss. There was an intensity to it that called to something inside her. She answered the challenge and matched his mood kiss for kiss, stroke for stroke, until he finally rolled her underneath him and entered her with a gentleness that made her want to weep. And when it was over, they lay still, Micah behind her, his palm stroking up and down her arm.

He kissed her neck and nibbled her ear before rolling her over to face him. "Hey, I want to tell you something, okay?"

Her heart seized in her chest. Was he

going to say what she thought he was? That he loved her?

"Yes, of course."

"I told you I know how it is to feel truly alone. I want you to know I wasn't just saying that."

"Okay." She blinked. This was not what she'd expected, but she sensed something important was going to follow his words.

"I told you my parents and I had some differences, but there was a lot more to it than that." His hand came out and touched her face, stroked down her nose, his thumb trailing across her lips. "You're so beautiful, did you know that? So perfect."

She stiffened slightly before forcing herself to relax. This wasn't about her. It was about him.

"Tell me about your parents."

His fingers retreated, and he reached down to grip one of her hands. "When I was really little, the woman I thought was my mom left and another woman came and took her place. Only that woman hadn't been my mom. Nor was the next. She was one in a long succession of nannies. Each of them was the first person I saw when I got up and the last person I saw when I went to bed. I knew other people lived in the house, but I rarely saw them."

He gave a rough laugh. "Later on I realized these people who slid in and out of rooms were actually my parents. Parents who seemed to avoid me."

"Oh, Micah, how terrible. Did they never interact with you?"

"They tried periodically, but it always seemed half-hearted. I remember one time I was six or seven, a friend came and knocked on the door. My mom answered and actually thought the kid was me standing there. She asked him why he was knocking at his own house."

Lia's heart turned ice-cold even as she forced herself to continue listening. That could have been her, mistaking his friend for her own child.

"I felt totally invisible, totally alone, like they could look at me and not really *see* me. It was as if I were simply living in their house, eating their food, sleeping in a bed they'd bought for some faceless individual. Now I realize that wasn't true, that of course they knew who I was. But back then?" He sighed and squeezed her hand. "It's really hard to have a relationship with people who I felt saw me as a generic human being. Kind of like a Mr. Potato Head doll with inter-changeable parts."

The sick feeling in Lia's stomach grew. So she was going to reveal to this man that to her people really were figures with inter-changeable features? If she ever had a child, was this how they'd feel? If a neighbor's kid came to the door, she actually might call him or her by her own child's name. Hadn't that happened with acquaintances who'd she'd called the wrong name and then covered it up with a laugh? Only seeing it through a child's eyes, Micah's eyes, it was a terrible, scarring truth that he would never, ever for-get. One that still ate at him even as an adult.

She did not want that for her child. But maybe Micah wouldn't want children. Maybe she could tell him her fears and he would wave them away, saying it wasn't a problem. They would just enjoy Lia's nieces.

And if he wanted kids?

"I can't imagine growing up like that. Why didn't you tell me this?"

"I think I was embarrassed. I eventually realized that my family wasn't like other families. And it most definitely wasn't like yours."

She sighed. "My family wasn't perfect, believe me."

"Maybe not. But at least they knew who you were."

Yes, they did. The problem was that without help, she hadn't always known who they were.

"Did you ever talk to them about how they made you feel?"

"No. But I should have. I should have been honest with them at some point."

Well, he wasn't the only person who hadn't been honest with those around him. Maybe it was time. If he realized she didn't want to be like his parents, but that in some ways she might end up acting like them without meaning to... Then what? He would just be like, *Okay, not a problem?*

Maybe she could tackle this from a different angle. "Well, you certainly know what *not* to do as a parent."

He reached out and gripped her hand. "You know, I didn't want children—had convinced myself I'd be the worst parent imaginable, with the role models I had. But now I'm not so sure."

"You're not?" She swallowed, a chill coming over her. "The subject of kids barely came up when we were together."

"I know. I was afraid my decision not to have them might scare you off. But now..."

Well, in the hospital that day when Sassy came in, I held her, and as I looked down into her face, something twisted inside me. A kind of emotion that I've only felt once before in my life." He carried her palm up to his mouth and kissed it, his lips warm on her cold skin. "I think with the right partner— one who knows how just how important it is to make people feel special—I might re-consider. *If* that partner is willing to take a chance on me, that is."

He was talking about her? She almost laughed aloud. It should be the other way around. She should be asking him if he was willing to take a chance on her. A sense of panic began to rise up inside her. He had no idea who he was talking to.

Her resolution to tell him the truth shat-tered into a million pieces as she looked at this man she loved more than life itself. A man she'd loved enough to give up once be-fore. And now?

She didn't know. Maybe she was look-ing at this scene through eyes that couldn't see the whole picture. But the portion of it that she could see—that of a young child who felt so totally invisible to those who should have loved him—tore at her heart and caused a pain she wasn't sure she could withstand. Wasn't sure she could take the risk of becoming *that* parent: the one who couldn't see what was right in front of her.

Dio ti prego aiutami.

Her silent prayer for help brought no answers. And she couldn't bear to contemplate the subject anymore. So she murmured, "Tell me more about your life as a child."

Maybe Micah would somehow lead her to the answer she so desperately needed.

So as he continued to open up, she let him talk, making sympathetic noises whenever there was a lull in the conversation. But the iciness that had started in her heart slowly encased her in a prison she felt there was no escape from.

Finally Micah was all talked out, and he reached for her again. She held him. Kissed him. Loved him. Hopefully, by morning, she would have her decision and have the strength to carry it out. Once and for all.

Micah woke up in the morning feeling refreshed in a way he hadn't felt in a very long time. He'd poured out his heart to Lia. The very first person he'd ever shared that with. He sucked down a deep breath and smiled.

Hell, he loved the woman. Wanted to be with her. Wanted to have children with her.

When she looked at him, there was no feeling of invisibility.

Speaking of Lia, she wasn't in bed. Maybe she was taking a shower. He rolled out from beneath the covers, finding that ridiculous robe and pulling it on. He ventured out into the hall. The bathroom door was open, and when he went into the kitchen, she was there bent over a basket of laundry, folding it. Her back was to him, but he recognized his slacks. A feeling of warmth went through him.

"Hi, there. You didn't have to do my laundry."

Lia whirled around, holding the pants in front of her almost as if they were some kind of shield. That was ridiculous. Of course she wasn't. He'd just startled her.

"Sorry. I didn't mean to scare you."

"You didn't." She added his trousers to a small stack of clothing. "I think they should all be dry by now."

Her words and movements were quick and flighty, like a bird peck, peck, pecking at the ground and picking up anything it could find. He went to touch her, but she moved away, making it seem like an accident, as if she didn't know what he'd been trying to do. But that initial flinch said otherwise.

What was going on? Last night she hadn't been able to get enough of him, and this morning… Well, if they'd been at his hotel room he could almost guarantee that she'd already be out of there.

He took a step closer. "Are you okay?"

"Fine. I just need to be at work in about a half hour."

"I'm sorry, you should have woken me."

She smiled, but the curve of lips didn't reach her eyes. "I figured you could let yourself out once you got up."

Ah, so it didn't matter if they were at his place or hers. She was still going to run. Just like she had at graduation, when she said they weren't meant to be together.

Maybe he was reading too much into this. It could be she was telling him the truth. Maybe she really did need to be at work and she was just trying not to be late.

"Okay, how about tonight?"

"Tonight?"

He swallowed. "Do you want to get together?"

Her teeth came down on her lip in that way that drove him crazy, only this time, it didn't. Because something strangely familiar was climbing up his chest and settling there, its spiny surface digging deep.

When she didn't answer him, he nodded, suddenly feeling just as alone as she'd said she felt the previous night. He could stand here and try to get her to open up until he was blue in the face, but something told him she wasn't going to tell him anything. Even after everything he'd told her last night.

"You don't want to, do you? Get together."

A shimmer of moisture appeared in her eyes as she slowly shook her head. "Micah, I am so, so sorry."

He hadn't been overreacting. She was taking the last page from their book and inserting it into their current chapter. And no matter what he might do or say, their story was going to end exactly the same way—with them going their separate ways.

He'd already had this particular dance with this woman, and he was damned if he was going to draw it out any longer than he had to.

"You're right. I would have seen myself out."

He pulled in a deep breath and drummed up the courage to be the one who said the goodbyes this time. "Sorry for unloading on your last night. I think we were both cold and tired and said some things we might not normally have said."

"It's okay."

It wasn't. But maybe someday in the far distant future, it would be. But this time he wasn't going to head to a bar and get flat-faced drunk. He was going to go to the hospital and do his job. He was going to see this pertussis crisis through, and then he was going to sit down and reevaluate his life. He needed to stay here for a while and sort through things with his parents. But after that?

He didn't know. But what he did know was that he wasn't going to let someone make him feel invisible ever again.

And he wasn't going to do this the way she had, simply severing ties. He was going to run this race all the way to the finish line, setting the pace for any future interactions.

His brows went up. "How's your ankle?"

"A little stiff, but it'll be fine."

"Good to hear." He took another step toward goodbye. "I'm planning on going out to hang up the rest of the signs this afternoon, but I can manage that on my own."

This time, she hesitated for a split second before saying, "Okay. Thank you."

And that, it seemed was that. So now he was going to make it very clear. He walked up to her and picked up his pile of clothes.

"I know you have to be at work, so I'll make this short. We'll probably run into one another at work, but I won't make things any more uncomfortable than they have to be. I'll be staying in Nashville for a while longer for my parents."

Her teeth dug into her lower lip again, but this time there was no core meltdown inside him. Just a sad tiredness that wanted this over and done.

"I hope things work out for you in life, Lia, I really do."

Her hands gripped the counter as if needing its support to remain upright before she whispered, "Thank you."

"Okay. I'll get dressed and get out of your hair, then."

With that he took his clothes and, without another look back, headed for her bathroom. Unsurprisingly by the time he was came out again, Lia was long gone. All that was left was Sam, her cat, pacing back and forth in front of the door with a pitifully soft meow. When she saw him, she hurried over, rubbing against his legs. He squatted down in front of her. "I know, girl. But there's nothing more I can do. So it seems this is goodbye."

The last thing he wondered as he locked her door and shut it behind him was how the hell she'd gotten to the hospital without her car.

CHAPTER THIRTEEN

GUAC AND TALKS WAS A pitiful affair. Lia had
put Avery off for three weeks before finally
agreeing to go. But by the end, her friend
hugged her and ordered her to go and deal
with the thing that was bothering her. It was
as if she'd known exactly what that thing
was. Or who.

Micah had made it pretty clear that this
time their breakup was permanent. Well, in
his defense, she'd kind of beaten him to the
punch, opting not to tell him the truth, just
like the last time they'd been together.

But it was as if Micah had probed her
deepest, darkest fears and stood them up in
front of her, saying, "This was how my life
was." And when he took her hand and mentioned having kids—implying she was the
person he'd choose to have them with—it
had been her undoing. The panic from that
time long ago, when she couldn't recognize

her own dad, had taken her down, paralyzing her.

Dio, the man had poured out his heart and soul to her, and the next morning she'd acted just like the people in his story. She'd barely spoken a word to him other than to say she was sorry. She'd never even told him what the hell she was sorry for.

And it wasn't fair.

Not to Micah, and not to her. But what other answer was there? He'd grown up not feeling seen by anyone in his life. And here was someone who was incapable of seeing him. Not because she didn't want to see him. But because she *couldn't*, dammit. She couldn't!

There was a huge difference between not wanting to and not being able to. But wasn't the end result the same? The odds were that she would one day call him or someone near him by the wrong name. Just like his mom had done to him. How could she live with herself if she did that?

How could she raise a child and have any different outcome than Micah had had?

The questions rolled around and around inside her, and then the loop started all over again.

She plopped into her chair at work and opened a file, staring at it, but not seeing it.

She'd seen her artwork all over town. Micah had indeed hung the flyers by himself. And in the end, his and the CDC's strategy seemed to be working. They were having record numbers of people coming in for their vaccinations, and the new reports of pertussis were beginning to wane.

She had acted terribly when Micah came out of the bedroom.

That had been wrong. So wrong. He'd deserved the truth that day, and she hadn't given it to him. He deserved to know *why* she thought their relationship was doomed.

At graduation, Micah had asked for an explanation, and she hadn't given it to him. This time he hadn't asked. He'd basically told her, "Never mind. I don't need to know. To hell with you."

The thing was, he wasn't the one who'd sent her to hell. She'd sent herself. Time after time. Relationship after relationship, whether it be girlfriends or high school boyfriends. She'd sabotaged every one of them in order to keep her secret. She had very few friends outside of Avery, because no one else could survive the freezing temperatures that came with inhabiting her world.

You owe him an explanation, Lia.
Why?

She already knew why. The man had shared his darkest moments with her, had told her things about himself that she'd never known.

Why now, when he hadn't the last time they were together?

He'd said it was because he was embarrassed.

But maybe it was because he'd finally trusted someone enough to tell them. And that someone had been her. And what had she done? By being unwilling to become just as vulnerable as he'd been, she'd batted his revelation away like it was of no importance.

But it was. It was so very important.

She swallowed. She'd never trusted anyone that much. Ever.

Pushing away the chart, she realized she needed to trust or she would remain that scared woman who'd stood frozen in the middle of her kitchen, too petrified to let down her guard and live life.

Avery was right. She needed to deal with the thing that was bothering her. Or someday, when she least expected, it was going to deal with her.

What if Micah told her to get the hell out

of his office without even giving her a hearing? Then she needed to find someone else to tell. And she needed to keep on trying until there was no secret left to tell.

She climbed to her feet, picking up her cell phone and scrolling until she found his number. She should probably call rather than just barging into his office, right?

What would she do if she was in his shoes and had advance notice of his arrival?

She'd make sure she was long gone by the time he got there. Kind of like she'd done when Micah had gone to get dressed that morning.

Okay, then she needed to just go. If he wasn't there, she would camp outside his office until he finally did appear.

So she took the elevator to the third floor and made her way down the hallway until the very end. Then she stood in front of his door for a very long time, her heart quaking in her chest. Then she raised her hand and knocked. Hard enough for anyone within earshot to hear.

"Come in."

Dio, could she do it?

The fact was, she had to. She went into his office and found him up to his elbows in…boxes.

Panic swept through her. "You're leaving?"

"Yep."

"I thought you said you were staying in Nashville to help with your parents."

His brows went up, and there was a coolness to his eyes that made her want to cry out. "I'm not leaving Nashville. Or the hospital. But I am changing locations. The CDC liked our campaign and asked me to come on staff as a representative of Saint Dolly's."

"Oh." The wind went out of her sails.

"Did you need something?"

Her reason for coming here skittered back through her head at his words. Whether he stayed or whether he went was immaterial at this point. But she needed to be as honest with him as he'd been with her.

"I do. I need to talk to you for a minute, if you have the time."

For a second he looked like he might refuse, then he lifted some boxes off one of the chairs and motioned for her to sit. Whew. At least she wasn't going to have to do this standing up, because she wasn't sure her legs would support her.

Micah didn't take another seat, however, he stood over her, a hip leaning on his desk. It was disconcerting, as if he were trying to subtly convey that he didn't want her here and wasn't going to do anything to make her stay more comfortable.

Well, it was working.

"So what is it?"

She'd kind of thought this would go differently. That they'd both be sitting across from each other where she could watch his body language. But where he was didn't change what she was here for.

"You remember when you told me you felt invisible to your mom and dad? That you felt like some faceless entity? A Mr. Potato Head with interchangeable parts, I think you said?"

He shrugged. "I never should have told you any of that."

"*Dio*, Micah, yes, you should have. Because you hit my deepest dilemma on the head. You nailed the reason I broke things off with you all those years ago, and why I couldn't quite face you the last time we were together."

"I don't understand."

"I know you don't. And I should have told you all this at graduation. But I was… I was too afraid. I've been afraid all my life."

"You?"

"Yes." She looked down at her hands, twining her fingers together. This was it. It was now or never. "People's…faces…they, well, they don't register with me. I see them. I look at you and can see your face as plain as day. But when I look in the mirror, I see the same thing. A face. When I look at Arnie Goff, I see…a face." Her gaze came back up. "But they're indistinguishable from each other. They're Mr. Potato Heads."

He was looking at her like he had no idea what she was talking about.

She tried a new tack. "Ever hear of a condition called prosopagnosia?"

Something in his eyes clicked, and he frowned. "Face blindness? It's extremely rare."

She pointed her thumbs back at herself. "Dr. Micah Corday, meet Extremely Rare."

He tipped the chair next to hers, dumping the contents onto the ground, then turned it so he sat across from her. "You have prosopagnosia? You've had it the whole time we've known each other?"

"I've had it since I was an infant. I had a stroke that affected that part of my brain."

"So when you didn't recognize me at the Valentine's Day benefit…" His eyes closed. "Hell, I thought you didn't remember me."

"Oh, I remembered you. There's a huge

difference between recognizing and remembering."

"But how did you finally realize it was me?"

Lia looked at him. "You opened your mouth, and *you* poured out of it. And I normally recognized you." She reached out and touched his face. "Your dimple. The color of your eyes. The way your hair falls over your forehead. There are a thousand things about you that tell me it's you." And she loved every one of those things. Would always love them.

"So why did you break things off?"

This was hard. And real. And scary. She wasn't sure she could make it through the explanation without falling completely apart. "Everyone was in their caps and gowns that day. I looked over the crowd, and all I could see was a sea of orange and white. All the little indicators I used to tell people apart had suddenly been taken away. Including you. I panicked. One of my biggest fears was not being able to recognize my children, and a million moments ran through my head and I realized how many times we wear uniforms and ballet costumes and… caps and gowns."

"If you had told me…"

"It wouldn't have changed anything. That fear was...*is* still there. You described perfectly what any child born to me was going to experience. The sense of invisibility. Mistaking a neighbor's child for my own. You said you felt like a placeholder in your own home. That is the world *my* child will live in. And when you took my hand and said you wanted kids...with the right partner—" Her voice ended on a sob. One she swallowed down before it became a torrent. "I felt like absolutely the wrong person for you to do that with. You deserve so much better. You deserve to be seen. *Really* seen."

"Lia. No. That's not true. God, I had no idea how you would take any of that."

"I know. But it rang so true. It matched what I feared so perfectly."

He grabbed her hands and held them tight. "You say I deserve to be seen. Do you want to know how I felt when we were together back then? I *felt* seen for the first time in my life. Like you could peer inside me and see what no one else could. I felt like more than..." he smiled "...an indistinguishable set of parts. I felt whole and wanted."

"But you're an adult now. If I ever had a child—"

"If you ever *have* a child, he or she will

be very, very lucky. Can't you see? That little person will be known in a way that very few people will ever experience. What happened with my parents was willful and hurtful, even if they didn't mean it to be. I felt unwanted. Would yours feel like that?"

"No. Never." She lifted his hand and pressed it to her cheek. "I'm sorry, Micah. I should have told you. Back then. And when you were in my apartment that last time."

"That's why you acted so strange the next morning. You felt like you would doom your child to the life I was describing?"

She nodded.

"I should have seen it. Should have guessed you were struggling with something. If I had…"

"It's not your fault. The only person who has ever guessed the truth was Avery."

He smiled. "I can see how that might be. She's a good friend."

"Yes, she is."

He pulled in a breath and released it. "So where do we go from here?"

Something twitched in her belly. She hadn't been looking for anything more than to just tell him the truth. "What do you mean?"

"Did you break up with me because you didn't love me?"

"No, of course not."

He dragged her onto his lap and planted a hard kiss on her mouth. "Said as if that's a ridiculous thought. Well, it wasn't to me. You put me through hell, Lia."

"I didn't mean to. I was trying to save you. From me."

"What a misguided, unbelievable and totally incredible woman you are. But you didn't save me. You almost destroyed me." He cupped her face and looked into her eyes. "I have a very important question. You said you didn't break up with me for lack of love. Is that still true? That there's no lack of love?"

A veil lifted from her eyes, and she could see him clearly for the first time in her life. "There's no lack. I love you. I always have."

A muscle worked in his jaw. "What can I do to help you?"

"To help me? I don't understand."

"How can I help you believe that what you see when you look at me is enough? That it's always been enough." He smiled. "I have never felt invisible in your eyes."

"I believe you." Hope raged in her chest,

breaking free from the fear she'd carried with her from childhood.

"And you believe that your children...*our* children—maybe five or six?—will never feel invisible?"

She laughed. "Five or six? *Dio*, we may have to color code them. My mom always wore a pink crocheted bracelet on her wrist to help me spot her from a distance. She still does, although she probably doesn't need to anymore."

"There's your answer, then. If you're afraid, we'll have a different color bracelet for each child."

"We'll? Are you sure you want to—"

"Have children with you? Yes, and I'm hoping you feel the same way. I love you, Lia."

Love and belief swamped her heart, and she could finally envision a future where she could drop her guard and be herself.

In trusting Micah enough to tell him the truth, she'd given herself permission to be happy. And she was happy. Happier than she'd ever been. And she had a feeling life was only going to get better from here.

His kiss held a promise that didn't need facial recognition software to become reality. Because he'd told her he loved her just as she was. And so would their children. And this time—finally—Lia believed him.

EPILOGUE

Micah placed a pink crocheted bracelet around their baby's wrist, careful not to wake Lia, who was still sleeping after her difficult delivery.

Lia's mom had fashioned a tiny identification band that looked identical to the one she wore. It wouldn't have any information printed on it like you might expect on one of those kinds of bands, but it would serve as a tell, as she put it, the same way Micah's bright orange wedding band did. She'd sworn she didn't need him to wear anything more than a gold band, that she would always recognize him. But he wanted to. It was a sign that he supported his wife and would do anything he could to make things easier for her. And his band wouldn't be hidden under the sleeve of a coat the way a bracelet might.

He'd almost ruined things by not understanding why she'd withdrawn after their night together, and by not pressing her for answers. Once they figured things out, they'd sworn they would keep no more secrets from each other. Lia had gone to Arnie Goff as well and shared about her prosopagnosia, and he assured her it would have no effect on her job at the hospital.

As for his parents, he'd been surprised and pleased by their response to the news he was getting married. His mom had actually taken it upon herself to make the bridal bouquet and the one for Avery, who was Lia's matron of honor. Little inroads were being made every time he turned around, it seemed. And his dad's experimental cancer treatment was working better than expected. He hadn't gone into remission yet, but there was a very real possibility it would happen.

The only glitch had come when Lia found herself unexpectedly pregnant a month before they said their vows. It was her deepest fear and the reason she'd broken things off with him. He'd taken her in his arms and reassured her that their baby would not get lost in the shuffle. They would make it work. And with her mom and dad's help, they had.

"Hey, handsome." Lia's tired voice came

from the bed behind him, and he turned toward her. "Is she okay?"

"She's more than okay." He perched on the edge of the mattress. "How are you feeling?"

"Better."

Lia had developed preeclampsia in her thirty-eighth week of pregnancy, and because of the stroke she'd had as an infant, they'd decided rather than risk her blood pressure going any higher, they would deliver the baby. Fear had crawled up Micah's spine at the thought of losing Lia so soon after they'd found each other again, and when he'd been kicked out of the surgical suite, he'd found himself sitting in the hospital's chapel. There, with clasped hands resting on the chair in front of him, he'd poured his heart out to whomever in the cosmos might be listening. That's where the surgeon had found him a half hour later. And where he'd learned that both Lia and Chelsea Day Costa-Corday had made it. He would be forever grateful. And never would he take these two precious gifts for granted.

Micah stroked her damp hair back off her forehead. "You are my world—do you know that?"

She nodded. "Ditto, honey." She frowned and then put a hand on his arm. "I'm sorry. I forgot."

Surprisingly, the word didn't send his world spinning into chaos like it had that other time. Instead, it brought a sense of peace. "It's okay. I think it's growing on me. Especially since everyone in your family calls everyone honey. Well, in Italian."

"It's part of my heritage. I could use the Italian term if you'd rather."

"No. Although there are times when I really do like hearing you speak in your heart language. Like when you're cussing." He grinned and leaned closer. "Or when you're loving me."

"Micah!"

It was a huge turn-on when his wife was so caught up in the moment that she breathed words he didn't understand across his skin. Even thinking about it caused areas that should be quiet to wake up.

It would always be this way. He wanted this woman. Only this woman.

"Sorry. I can't help it."

She slid her finger down the left side of his face. "It's okay." Her eyes shifted to the clear bassinet a short distance away. "Can I hold her?"

"Of course." Micah helped her sit up and propped a pillow across the area where her incision was. Then he turned and reached into the bassinet and gingerly lifted their child, moving with careful steps until he reached her. Laying her in Lia's arms, he moved around to the other side of the bed and slid in beside her.

This was where he belonged. And this was where he would stay.

He saw her reach for their daughter's wrist and touch the bracelet. "Where...?"

"Your mom brought it in while they were doing the C-section."

She gathered her baby close, tears filling her eyes and spilling onto her cheeks. "I just never thought I'd be this lucky."

Micah kissed the top of her head, trying to banish the burning sensation behind his own eyes. "Luck? I don't think so. I think maybe your friend Avery was right."

"What do you mean?"

He leaned his cheek against her temple. "Remember when she was talking about Samantha?"

"Samantha? As in our cat?"

"Hmm... Yes, her little bell jingled on your key chain, and then Avery said you'd named her for her witchy ways."

"Well, 'witchy' was a nice way of putting it."

He laughed. "Well, be that as it may, contrary to her fierce reputation, she didn't exactly attack me that first night I met her."

"Unlike me on that same night." She sent him a look that told him exactly what she meant.

"Don't distract me. But even that kind of proves my point."

"Proves your point?" She tilted her head until it rested against his. "So are you somehow saying that Samantha had something to do with me sleeping with you that first night? With us getting together afterward?"

"Maybe. I'm forever hearing her little bell wandering around our house at night."

"And?"

"I swear I've seen her nose twitch a time or two when she looks at us."

Lia laughed, then her free hand came up and curved around his cheek, turning his face so she could kiss him. "You know, I think I've seen that, too. So you think Sam twitched her witchy little nose and cast a spell on us?"

"Are you denying it's a possibility?"

"No, and now that I think about it, she did kind of force her way into my heart at the shelter not long after I broke up with you. She helped me grieve your loss that first time. And she helped me work up the courage to tell you about my condition."

"That cat deserves a medal for making our problems vanish, if so."

"No. That cat deserved a family. And it looks like she got one. One that isn't going to disappear."

His arm tightened around her. "Good. Because I'm not going anywhere."

"That makes two of us. I love you, Micah."

As he stared down at his little family, his heart filled with love and gratitude. And then he glanced out the window at the skies and beyond and mouthed, "Thank you."

* * * * *